Praise for Hugh Mack

'Wildly original and thoroughly ~~........~~'
The Australian

'Unnerving and intense as it is, it is addictive reading.'
Sunday Mail

'Deftly and adroitly managed'
Australian Book Review

'His writing . . . illuminates not only the question of love
but the search for meaning . . . this makes him a rare
temperament in fiction.'
Arts Hub

'Accomplished, highly readable and blackly funny.'
Canberra Times

Hugh Mackay is a social psychologist and bestselling author. *The Therapist* is his ninth novel. His non-fiction writing covers social and cultural analysis, psychology, communication and ethics.

Hugh is a Fellow of the Australian Psychological Society and the Royal Society of New South Wales, and was appointed an officer of the Order of Australia in 2015. He lives in Canberra.

THE
THERAPIST

THE THERAPIST

HUGH MACKAY

ALLEN&UNWIN
SYDNEY·MELBOURNE·AUCKLAND·LONDON

Allen & Unwin
Cammeraygal Country
83 Alexander Street
Crows Nest NSW 2065
Australia
Phone: (61 2) 8425 0100
Email: info@allenandunwin.com
Web: www.allenandunwin.com

Allen & Unwin acknowledges the Traditional Owners of the Country on which we live and work. We pay our respects to all Aboriginal and Torres Strait Islander Elders, past and present.

 A catalogue record for this book is available from the National Library of Australia

ISBN 978 1 76106 835 5

Set in 13/17.98 pt Garamond Premier Pro by Midland Typesetters, Australia
Printed and bound in Australia by the Opus Group

10 9 8 7 6 5 4 3 2 1

TO SHEILA

Maybe, in the end, even the lies we tell define us. And better, some of them, than our most earnest attempts to tell the truth.

David Malouf, *Johnno*

ONE

ON A GREY DAY LIKE THIS, YOU WOULD HAVE BEEN CHEERED by the sight of Martha Elliott as she approached her consulting rooms—a converted cottage across the road from the bulky eastern side of Chatswood Chase shopping centre. Her handsome face radiated kindness, optimism and an eagerness to ease the pain of all those (well, almost all) who came to her for advice, support, guidance . . . or for nothing more than the comfort of her patiently listening ear. Perhaps for the reassurance that here was someone who was finally taking them seriously. Martha's green eyes might startle you at first, but her generous smile was always hovering, waiting to bestow its blessing on you.

Not that Martha was a soft touch. Some of her friends called her 'brisk', by which she knew they meant 'brusque'. Some clients discovered there was a limit to her patience, and were shocked by the directness of her response to their meandering, repetitive tales of woe. 'Empathy is my stock in trade,' Martha was fond of saying, 'but gullibility isn't. It would be a dereliction of my duty to let people drown in a sea of self-pity. We're here to make progress, not wallow.'

Feeling older than her sixty-seven years, long-since divorced, still bruised from a disastrous subsequent relationship with a younger man, mother of Samantha—single, forty, determined to get pregnant, partner or no partner—Martha greeted every day with relish. Even this dull, damp, midwinter Monday.

As she unlocked the front door of the cottage, she was suddenly struck by the sight of her brass plate on the wall—*Martha Elliott, Psychologist.* She paused and looked at it as if she were seeing it for the first time, then went inside and prepared her morning cup of coffee. She settled herself in the chair in her office and waited for another working week to begin, savouring this half-hour of solitude before her first appointment.

Knowing the end of this road was in sight, Martha had recently been pondering its beginning . . .

Fifty years ago, when she was finishing school and wondering what to do with her life, she had attended a local church where she would occasionally fantasise about becoming a curate. She knew there was no way a woman could have gone down that path—not then and, as far as Sydney Anglicans were concerned, possibly not ever. But she was intrigued by that archaic word 'curate'. The cure of souls; the care of souls. She felt the same little thrill when she heard someone being described as the curator of a museum or gallery collection—all that precious artwork gave the place its soul, she thought, and wasn't art itself an expression of the artist's soul? No wonder it needed a curator. A curate.

Her Church of England phase didn't survive first-year university. She found the Sydney Anglicans' obsession with people's sexual preferences repugnant. To her, it seemed as if they were more interested in sex than love. A couple of her gay friends were told in no uncertain terms that they were going to hell and there was no place for them in the church, so they left and Martha left with them. Her boyfriend, Simon, who became her husband, wouldn't have a bar of religion. Even at nineteen, he struck Martha as a shameless materialist. He even hated her telling him he had a biblical name.

But she never lost what those evangelical Anglicans had called the 'passion for souls'. Though her own passion became entirely secular, she was determined, from the very beginning, to help save troubled souls from themselves.

Once she got into clinical psychology, Martha felt she had found her true vocation. She loved it from the start, even though, looking back, she acknowledged that she used to say too much. Perhaps try too hard. She certainly felt, in retrospect, that she had been unduly influenced by Freud and his obsession with sex—a bit like those Sydney Anglicans. For Martha, Jung had hit the nail on the head when he accused Freud of replacing God with sexuality as the object of his worship. Still, some of her contemporaries were out-and-out Freudians and she had to admit he was a great storyteller (while also something of a scientific fraud) and, yes, he gave us 'the unconscious mind'. The label, at least—Martha liked to remind her Freudian friends that it was hardly an original idea. Creative artists, thinkers, mystics have always known about the unconscious mind, she insisted. Homer. Plato. Jesus. Shakespeare. Buried history. Hidden motives. Dark impulses. Saying one thing, even meaning it, and doing another. Unconsciously projecting our own faults and frailties on to others.

Martha's assessment of her own professional journey was that she had evolved into a hybrid. She liked to say that she 'mixed it up a bit'; even that she was something of a 'mongrel therapist'— a bit of this, a bit of that. She had added foot massage to her repertoire of therapies for some of her female clients, and she regarded that as no more than an extension of the direction she was already taking with breathing exercises and the occasional guided meditation: 'There's nothing like meditation to stimulate feelings of compassion in people who have been too dry for too long,' she assured her more sceptical colleagues.

Martha saw her responsibility as offering whatever kind of care a particular soul might need. She abhorred single-mindedness. Straight lines and tight boundaries. The One True Way. 'Oh, yes,' she would say, 'there's plenty of that in psychology as well as religion. "Doctrinaire" doesn't begin to describe it.'

Whenever Martha sank into pensive mode, regret about her marriage was never far from her thoughts. 'Married too early and divorced too late' was her summary of her marital history. Her daughter, Sam, was born when Martha was twenty-seven, and while her career was a bit slow to build momentum, she came to believe that that had been a very good thing: 'I needed to live a little. To spread my wings personally as well as professionally.'

As Sam grew up and Martha was able to get into a more regular working routine, she kept coming back to that idea of the care of souls; the cure of souls. She soon decided that the talking cure was wonderful, but it was not always the answer. Or not the only answer. Or not the whole answer. 'And, anyway,' she would often say, 'it really should be called the listening cure. Sometimes, people just need to be heard. Accepted. Understood. Or even just encouraged to be who they are. To take time out for some quiet reflection in a safe space.'

Martha sometimes wondered whether there was a better professional description of her than 'psychologist': 'So what should I call myself? What label fits me? I'm a counsellor, yes. I'm a reflexologist—well, not really. I did a course in reflexology, but I wasn't convinced by all the theory. I certainly accept that it can do no harm and might sometimes do a power of good. So let's just say

I dabble in foot massage. Well, more than dabble. I believe it can really enrich the therapeutic experience. It's more than relaxation. It opens people up. Helps them shed their inhibitions.'

She also regarded herself as an educator, though she complained that that had become an unfashionable word: 'These days, even at universities, it's all about "teaching and learning", as if everyone's afraid to utter the E word.' But Martha regarded it as a beautiful word, and she loved the idea of encouraging her clients to learn more about themselves. She loved being able to facilitate that process for them. To draw them out. Liberate them. Unleash them. Free them to explore their capacities. Their potential. Their truth. 'Education at its purest,' she would say of her work as a therapist.

Yet Martha was acutely conscious of the imperfections inherent in the therapeutic process: nothing was ever complete. No jigsaw was ever quite finished. She struggled constantly with the sense that she was only hearing part of every story. Where was the point of view of the other people—the people lurking just beyond the edge of her conversations with clients; the people who often seemed to be the source, or the focus, of a client's trouble?

Once, when Martha was describing this frustration to Robin Nielsen, her partner in the practice, she put it like this: 'When a client leaves my office, it's as if I can still feel their presence, and I say to that ghostly trace, "Yes, and what else?" Truly, I sometimes wonder if I'm in danger of being overwhelmed by all the things I don't hear.'

TWO

IN HER FORTY YEARS AS A COUNSELLOR—MINUS A YEAR off for some post-divorce wound-licking and another for bad behaviour—Martha had never experienced anything quite like this. It was to be her first session with Abigail and Bill Orton, a couple in their early fifties who seemed, from the moment they entered her office, to be gratingly ill at ease with each other. Their introductions had been perfunctory, they had talked over each other, and Martha thought a glance Abigail had shot at Bill was nakedly hostile.

Once the Ortons were settled in their chairs, Martha asked the open-ended questions she normally used at the beginning of a new client relationship. 'So Abigail, Bill, perhaps you'd like to tell me what brought you here today. How might I be of some help?'

The couple exchanged looks that Martha couldn't interpret. Then Bill sat back in his chair and Abigail leaned forward in hers.

'Before we talk about any of that,' Abigail said, 'there is one thing I need to clarify.'

'By all means, Abigail. What's on your mind?'

'If we go ahead with this, Bill and I will end up revealing some of the secrets of our marriage to you. Some of our . . . issues. Right, Bill?'

'Yeah. Sure. Definitely.'

'But you need to know that we're both a bit sceptical about psychotherapists. I've heard lots of horror stories, but I happen to know someone who's really quite familiar with your work, so I thought we might be on safer ground with you. But I need some reassurance.'

'What kind of reassurance?'

Abigail gazed intently at Martha. 'You know how you feel if you go to a doctor who's clearly obese but tries to give you advice about losing weight? You tend to be sceptical. You think there's a bit of—what? Hypocrisy? *Do as I say, not as I do.* That kind of thing. The god-doctor. But it's not only doctors, is it? I'm sure you'd be aware of the number of psychotherapists who come into that category. Very free with their advice. Very keen to interpret what's going on in other people's lives as if they alone hold the key to some deep inner truth. Sorry if that sounds offensive, but you know what I mean. The god-therapist. And then you find their own personal life is a shambles. Kids off the rails. Divorces. Affairs. Estranged from their families. Whatever. And you think, just like that unhealthy doctor, *Physician, heal thyself.* I mean, maybe they're good at their job, but not at their *life*. Do you get what I mean?'

'I do indeed, Abigail. But I'm not sure what you're asking me.'

Abigail sighed rather theatrically. 'Look,' she said, 'I don't deny there are stresses in our marriage. For a start, I would like Bill to speak up for himself a bit more. Bit of an invertebrate is Bill. I love him dearly, of course, but he needs to toughen up a bit. Be more robust.'

'Robust?'

'No, no . . . wait. My point is, I know you're fully qualified. I can see those certificates on your wall. But what does your *life* say? We want to be sure we're not placing ourselves in the hands of a hypocrite. Sounds a bit blunt, but there it is.'

'That's fine. But I think it's rather beside the point, Abigail, if you don't mind me saying so. If you're asking me if I'm some kind of saint, then no, of course I'm not. I have my share of human foibles and failings. But I am an experienced therapist. I mean, athletics coaches know how to get the best out of an athlete without necessarily being champion athletes themselves. Now perhaps you, or maybe Bill'—Martha turned to Bill, who was staring at the carpet—'might like to say a bit more about the issue you've just raised.'

Abigail, becoming increasingly agitated, shook her head defiantly. 'Not until you've dealt with *our* issue. When it comes to counselling, we think a therapist's professional integrity mainly depends on their *personal* integrity. Am I making myself clear?'

'You are, Abigail. But, really, my personal life simply doesn't come into it. I'm a professional person trained to help you clarify— perhaps resolve—whatever difficulties you and Bill might be dealing with. If you find my approach helpful, that's all that really matters, isn't it?'

Abigail was now rigid with tension. 'No, it's *not* all that matters. I'm obviously not making myself clear. It's *hypocrisy* I can't stand!'

As she said this, Abigail rose abruptly from her chair as if she'd had a sudden change of heart about coming here in the first place. She strode to the door, flung it open, marched out and slammed the door behind her

At precisely that moment, there was a furious thunderclap, closely followed by the sound of rain beating heavily on the windows. When Martha later tried to describe the moment to her colleague, she could hardly separate the sound of the slammed door from the thunderclap, as if nature had been supplying the soundtrack to Abigail's exit.

Martha and Bill listened in amazement to the sound of the Ortons' car starting, the wheels spinning briefly on the gravel driveway before the car reversed out into the street.

A moment later, they heard the thud and tinkle of a collision and the sound of a woman's voice, unmistakably Abigail's, shrieking obscenities. A man's voice, barely audible against the din of the rain and the shrieking, was also shouting.

'I'm sorry about this. I'd better go and see what's happened,' Bill said.

Martha went to the window and watched as Bill hurried down the driveway, hunched over against the driving rain, then paused on the footpath to assess the scene. Abigail appeared through the rain and threw herself against him. Bill put his arms around her and they stood there, sodden, rather like a sculpture in a fountain whose water spray had gone berserk.

Shaking her head in amazement, Martha sat down and reflected on what had just happened. The most likely explanation for Abigail's abrupt departure, she thought, was that she was trying to postpone any serious confrontation with the issues in their marriage that had led them to contact Martha. Perhaps the therapy had actually been Bill's idea and the stuff Abigail was saying about his spine needing stiffening was mere cover; a way of easing into therapy without full disclosure. It wouldn't be the first time.

But there was another issue niggling at Martha. She prided herself on the reliability of her built-in lie detector, and that whole encounter had seemed to her to be inauthentic, almost like a scripted performance. Her exposure to them had been so fleeting, she couldn't hazard a guess at what lie might be lurking in the shadows of the Orton story, though she was certain there was one.

She scribbled a few notes and then went into the reception area, where Sandrine was at her most enigmatic.

Receptionist, practice manager and general factotum, but also friend and confidante to Martha and Rob, Sandrine had been there since the day Martha started her own practice, twenty years ago. They were almost the same age, though Sandrine was always immaculately dressed and coiffed, in sharp contrast to Martha's more relaxed appearance. Clients loved Sandrine and sometimes spilled their secrets to her while they were waiting for a session with Martha or Rob. Sandrine had recently become a grandmother for the second time and, like Martha, was beginning to talk about retirement.

'I wonder if we'll ever be paid for that session,' Sandrine said with a grim smile. 'Oh, and your eleven o'clock is running late— caught in the storm, obviously. He's another newbie.'

Martha looked at her watch. 'I'm not worried about being paid for today, but I do rather wonder if we'll hear from them again. I certainly hope so.'

'Really? I thought she was a very odd woman, that one.'

Martha raised her eyebrows. Her hope that the Ortons would return was only partly based on her professional desire to help someone as agitated as Abigail appeared to be; she also disliked unsolved mysteries.

'Does Rob have anyone with him at present?' she asked.

'All clear,' Sandrine said, extending her open palm towards the passage that led to the rear of the cottage.

Meanwhile, Abigail was in the back of a taxi with Bill, sending a text.

Hi Gabs
We have lift-off. Ruined my exit by crashing the car.
Talk tonight?
Abs xox

> *Great news. R u ok? Won't tell Himself till the death.*
> *Call after 10. He'll be out cold by then. Gabs xox*

THREE

ROBIN NIELSEN—UNIVERSALLY KNOWN AS ROB—HAD BEEN Martha's professional partner for fifteen years. Despite their many differences of opinion and radically different approaches to the practice of psychotherapy, they were firm friends as well as colleagues. She walked the few steps to his office, knocked, paused, then opened the door. Rob looked up, frowning.

'What's wrong?' Martha asked.

'Constancia has been screaming at me on the phone. Questioning my devotion. Threatening to end it all. Again. Still.'

Martha perched herself on the edge of Rob's desk. 'Oh?' she replied, smiling.

'Don't smirk,' Rob said.

Martha raised her eyebrows. 'That was a smile, not a smirk. I can do a proper smirk if you'd like me to.'

'No thanks. I know a smirk when I see one and believe me, that was a smirk. Look, I know Constancia isn't your favourite person. She's not mine either right now, to tell you the truth. But cut me a bit of slack. Where's that famous Martha Elliott empathy?'

'Do you want me to react as your counsellor, your colleague or your friend?'

Rob slumped in his chair, his hands gripping his thighs and his gaze fixed on the ceiling. Martha thought, as she often had over the years, that he was a remarkably good-looking fellow. Well over six feet tall, with greying fair hair, clear blue eyes and olive skin that seemed perpetually tanned, he still had a springy, athletic look about him in spite of the slight paunch that had appeared recently. Martha still referred to him as 'my young colleague', though he had recently turned fifty. She knew there was a brief marriage buried in his distant past, but it perplexed her that a man with all Rob's attractive qualities should have become involved with a woman as deeply disturbed as Constancia.

'Sorry, Rob. You know I'm sympathetic. If you were my client, I'd probably ask you to tell me the story from Constancia's point of view. Imagine what's going on inside her troubled mind. Then we could put some kind of frame around the situation and see what we have to work with. I can't imagine you're in the mood to give that a try. Forgiveness is probably a bit out of reach right now, too. Am I right?'

Rob looked at Martha sharply. 'Forgiveness? What do I have to forgive Constancia for? If anything, I need her to forgive me.'

'For?'

Shrugging as if he were worn out by this entire saga, Rob said nothing.

'Believe it or not, Rob, I was talking about forgiving yourself. If you're interested, I can tell you *why* I think you need to forgive yourself.'

'Good try, Martha. Maybe some other time. As usual, I'm being cast as the bad guy here. It might even be true. She's accusing me of no longer having my heart in the relationship, and she might even be right. Anyway, if Constancia won't forgive me for whatever I'm supposed to have done this time, it'd be a bit pointless forgiving myself.'

'Alright. If you were the therapist, what would *you* say?'

Rob lifted his gaze to meet Martha's. There was a long pause.

'I think I'd say, "You need to get that mad bitch out of your life before you go completely bonkers yourself."'

Martha applauded silently. 'If only,' she said. 'If only we had the guts to say something like that when it really does need to be said. Doesn't your patience sometimes wear thin?'

'With Constancia? Regularly. But clients? We'd be cactus if we ever let something like that slip out. Imagine.'

'Ah, well. A pleasing fantasy.'

Martha eased herself off the edge of Rob's desk and sat in the chair his clients normally occupied. This was clearly not the moment to mention the little Orton drama. 'Speaking of pleasing fantasies, is the prospect of getting Constancia out of your life forever mere fantasy? Or is it real? If she is threatening to leave you yet again, why don't you just let her go? What's holding you back? What are you afraid of?'

'What would I be afraid of?' Rob appeared to consider this. 'Loneliness? I don't think so. More like liberation. A sense of failure? Yeah, maybe. The thought of her finding someone else too quickly? I'm not that pathetic—or that unrealistic. No, it's more that . . . . I'm not sure how to put this. Constancia was—don't mock me—she was my gold standard. I really thought she was the most remarkable woman I'd ever met. In fact, I once thought she was the most remarkable *person* I'd ever met.'

'Oh, Rob. Really? *Really?* And what would you say to a client who served up that kind of tosh?'

'Fuck off, Martha.'

For almost two years, Rob's tempestuous relationship with Constancia had been upsetting his equilibrium and eroding his self-confidence—even his self-respect, Martha feared. She was impatient with his talk of loving Constancia; everything about the relationship signalled raging lust and nothing more. Not that Martha was against lust, but having been badly burned by its flames herself, she wished there was a way to help Rob see past it. As things stood, he didn't even seem to be getting any fun out of the affair.

She walked to the door, paused, and said: 'You once told me Constancia has two sisters who are devoted to her. She has friends. Colleagues. She'll be absolutely fine on her own, Rob. And she wouldn't be on her own for long, anyway—Constancia is not the fiercely independent spirit she makes herself out to be. She needs playmates. Or worshippers, anyway. No, I'm not the slightest bit worried about Constancia. It's *you* I'm worried about. Sometimes I struggle to find the Rob I knew, BC.'

Aware that she'd already said too much, Martha had one more thing to add. 'You know, I wonder about people like us. You *and* me. Are we destined to fall in love with—or at least lust after—damaged people? People we think we can save?'

She looked at Rob for a reaction, but he was gazing at the carpet.

'Sorry, Rob, but you really are hanging on as if she's a client you have some responsibility for. You're not her therapist, though Lord knows she needs one. She is not your responsibility. Not when she's apparently the one who wants to split. You don't even have to broach the subject. She's handing it to you on a plate. Can you do it? *Liberation*—that was your word. Imagine the feeling, Rob. Imagine the relief.'

Only silence from Rob.

Martha left, closing the door quietly behind her.

Martha kept her deepest reservations about Constancia to herself, but her heart frequently bled for Rob. She had sometimes wondered whether he was actually addicted to Constancia's attention, even when it took the form of flagrantly manipulative—even coercive—behaviour. More than one of Martha's clients had mistakenly interpreted manipulation for attentiveness, drawing the sadly misguided conclusion that at least someone was taking notice of them. In fact, for a man who otherwise seemed so sane and stable, addiction struck Martha as the kindest explanation of Rob's persistence in the face of such discouragement. She reminded herself that gamblers, too, remained addicted in spite of multiple discouragements. She found it hard to imagine what might have to happen for Constancia's grip on Rob to be broken. Even the appeal of other women seemed as lost on him as the appeal of lemonade to an alcoholic.

'Your eleven o'clock will be here in ten minutes,' Sandrine said as Martha passed through the waiting room. 'And Sam called. Can you please ring her back? It sounded kind of urgent.'

⁓

For a minute or two after Martha had left his office, Rob remained in his chair, head in hands. Then he went to the door, locked it, and returned to his desk. He took his mobile phone out of his pocket and scrolled through his messages. A dozen texts from Constancia, all received in the few minutes he had been talking to Martha, the messages progressively briefer and more urgent. He jabbed her number.

'Constancia? Where are you? . . . No, I was just talking to Martha about a problem client . . . Yeah, I know . . . Yeah, you could be right, she could be losing her . . . Yeah, I agree, but let's not go over all that yet again . . . No, of course not . . . No, I didn't mean it like that, Constancia. There's no way that's going to happen . . . Anyway, I can't really talk now—I'm expecting a client any minute. Let's discuss it when we both get home, okay? . . . Lunch? Today? Oh. I . . . No, I do, I do . . . Where? Okay, I'll book . . . Oh, will you? That'd be great . . . Yeah, me too.'

FOUR

MARTHA'S ELEVEN O'CLOCK APPOINTMENT LOOKED TO HER to be only recently out of school, but his information form said he was thirty-two, married, with a three-year-old child. Working for an online data analysis company. Tall. Gangly. Neatly trimmed ginger hair. Fashionable stubble. Uniquely among Martha's current crop of clients—and very unusually, in Martha's experience, for an IT person—he was wearing a suit and tie. He was also looking very uncomfortable about being there. Martha assumed this appointment was not his idea, and so she adopted an approach she often used with reticent or anxious clients.

'Hello, Lucas. I'm Martha. It's good to meet you. Please take a seat.' She paused for a moment and smiled at this rather earnest-looking young man who was avoiding eye contact. 'Now, before we get started, let's just do a bit of deep breathing together. Okay? Close your eyes.'

Under Martha's guidance, and with obvious reluctance, Lucas complied.

'That was good. I'm a great believer in not rushing things. So . . . feeling okay? Good. Well then, why don't you tell me a bit about how you come to be here today?'

As if it were a prepared speech, and apparently undeterred by the pause for deep breathing, Lucas plunged in. 'My marriage. I'm here about my marriage. My friend Matt—we work together at Baessler-Johns Analytics—BJA—anyway, Matt said if you've got a sore tooth, you go to the dentist, right? If you've got a rattle in your car, you go to a mechanic. Well, I've got a sore marriage, I guess, or maybe there's a rattle in there somewhere. So that's why I'm here.' He paused and looked at Martha as if he'd temporarily lost his train of thought. 'I must admit I feel a bit . . . well, I've never done anything like this before. It's certainly not like the dentist, is it?'

Lucas smiled nervously and glanced quickly around the room, as if to check no one else was listening.

'Sore in what way, Lucas?'

'The thing is . . . well the thing is empathy. Loss of. Highly ironic, really, considering I've always said, right from the get-go, that I would prioritise empathy. I would rank empathy as a KPI in my marriage.'

'And does your wife understand that sort of talk—KPIs and so on?'

'Oh, yes. KPIs. Key performance indicators. She's worked in corporate HR ever since uni. We met on the job. At a BJA offsite, actually. She was doing a PowerPoint presentation. A roadmap for boosting staff morale. Love at first slide, we used to say. We don't use that word so much now, barely four years on. I thought it would last longer than four years. Is that normal?'

'Normal?'

'I mean, the l-word fading like that after four years. And . . . well, the loss of empathy.'

'Yours or hers?'

'Hard to say. I mean, in a relationship like a marriage, isn't it reasonable to expect a bit of reciprocity? Isn't it a bit like being in love? I mean, you can't be *in love* all on your own, can you? Besotted, maybe, but not in love. Same thing with empathy. If you're the only one doing it, there's scope for a certain amount of empathy fatigue. Am I right?'

'Would you like to say something more specific about that loss of empathy? Where you see the signs of it, perhaps?'

'Well, let's see. How can I put this?' Lucas drew a scrap of paper from his trouser pocket and glanced at it. Then he looked at Martha rather quizzically, as if wondering whether he should proceed with his plan.

He cleared his throat, gave another nervous grin, and began speaking in a way that sounded to Martha like a presentation at a staff meeting. 'At BJA we like doing little exercises where we try to quantify everything. Just like we do with consumer online behaviour. Know what I mean? So Matt and I have been working out the factors that might contribute to an empathy index.'

'Go on, Lucas. I'm intrigued.'

'Things like smile-to-frown ratios. Frequency and degree of touching. Active versus passive listening. Minutes-per-day of eye contact. That kind of thing. Then there's the carnality factor, of course. That'd have to be core in a marriage, surely. On a ten-point scale, down from 3.7 to 0.8 in the last two years. A significant drop, on any analysis. That's a big contributor to the declining empathy index. Gotta be.'

Martha could not hide her astonishment. Startled by the very idea of Lucas trying to quantify empathy, she wondered if he and his colleagues were familiar with Einstein's famous remark about quantification.

'Not everything that counts can be counted, Lucas, and not everything that can be counted counts.'

'Hey! I like that, Martha. Was that off the top of your head?'

'I wish I could say yes. But no, Einstein got there first.'

Lucas smiled and nodded. 'I'll make a note of it.'

He whipped out his mobile phone and, thumbs flying, recorded the quote. Meanwhile, that jokey reference to a carnality factor had dragged Martha's unwilling mind back to an episode in her own past; to a time when a man she had loved made such heavy sexual demands on her that, according to Lucas's calculations, their carnality score would have been a perfect ten. But that was certainly not a sign of empathy. Quite the reverse. It was a sign of a needy neurotic for whom sex was an obsession. Martha shuddered inwardly at the recollection.

She tried to rearrange the expression on her face to appear impassive, but Lucas had picked up the vibration.

'Don't take this too literally,' he said. 'I'm being pseudo-scientific, of course. As I say, we fool around with this sort of stuff at BJA all the time. It's like a game, really. It probably sounds as if I'm not taking this seriously enough . . .'

A game *and* a great hiding-place, Martha thought. Another quote came to mind—*Lies, damned lies and statistics*. Was that Benjamin Disraeli? Anyway, Lucas's pseudo-statistics looked like a very effective way of avoiding engagement with the real issue.

'Not at all,' she said. 'I get the idea. But . . . *carnality*?'

'Sex, Martha' Lucas said, as if she needed the term explained. 'Frequency, intensity, duration of.'

Martha looked into Lucas's intense blue-grey eyes, shining behind steel-rimmed spectacles. Just beneath the surface of his awkwardly playful manner, she detected a very serious, very smart and very badly wounded young man.

'Lucas, I'm not sure that—'

Lucas put his scrap of paper back in his pocket. 'It's okay, Martha. Let's not get hung up on the stats. Or the semantics. That's another factor driving our empathy index down, by the way.'

'What is?'

'Rani says I get too hung up on semantics. I admit there is a bit of that going on these days. Arguing over the right word. Like *babysitting*. Ha! Rani caught me on the phone telling Matt I wouldn't be able to meet him and a few other mates one night because I had to babysit. You should have heard the commotion over that! "This is our child, Lucas! You can't babysit your own kids. You babysit *other* people's kids." Lucas shook his head, as if bewildered all over again. 'It was just a manner of speaking—not exactly the right word, but we all knew the intended meaning. Bottom line: not available to go out.'

'Any other examples of that kind of thing?'

'Oh, heaps. Where do you want me to start? Empathic versus empathetic—that's rather relevant, isn't it? Or perhaps the never-ending argument about uninterested versus disinterested? I'm certain I'm on the right side of that particular skirmish, by the way, even though Rani doesn't really seem to care much either way.'

'Actually, we might put that on hold for a moment. I haven't heard much about your wife's feelings in all this. Rani, is it? Would you like to try putting yourself in Rani's shoes? What do you think she might say if she was the one talking to me now?'

'Rani? God. Search me. She'd probably say I'm an under-performing unit. Something like that. Disappointing ROI.' Then, at Martha's questioning look, 'Return on investment? I assumed you'd know that one. She sometimes refers to me as an asset, by which she doesn't mean what you might think. She means a piece of exploitable equipment. Anyway, there's no way she'd be here talking to you. For someone in HR, she has a remarkably low tolerance threshold when it comes to this kind of psychology. Not in her wheelhouse at all. Rani is a behaviourist through and through. No time for anything as fancy as the mind. *All that mentalist rubbish*, she calls it . . . Lucas looked at his watch. 'So, anyway, what's the drumbeat?'

'The drumbeat?'

'You know. The drum. The modus operandi. The arrangements. How do you want to play this?'

'You mentioned *this kind* of psychology. Can you say a bit more about what you think this kind of psychology is?'

'You tell me. This was all Matt's idea, remember. I'm thinking . . . well, the opposite of the way Rani thinks about it. I'd be thinking . . . the *mind*? Sorting out what's going on behind the scenes? Not madness. I don't mean madness. I'm not mad. Not even Rani would say I'm mad. It's just, well . . . *anxiety*? I'm anxious a lot of the time. At least I think I am. Sweaty palms. Headaches. Overthinking stuff. Too eager for Rani to smile at me. Which she seems to have given up doing.'

There was a long silence. Lucas looked out the window at the rain still falling steadily. Then he looked around the room— the Jeffrey Smart prints on the wall, the tiny Margaret Preston original, Martha's professional certificates, the bookcase, the potted cyclamen—and finally back at Martha.

'So, what do you think? Is that enough to go on?'

'Lucas, I'm going to ask you to do something a bit unusual. Would you mind taking off your shoes?'

'My shoes? What, now?'

'Yes, right now, if you don't mind. It's just a little experiment I sometimes like to conduct with my clients. You'd be surprised how it can change the way you feel. Frees things up a bit. Give it a try.'

Looking embarrassed, almost as if he'd been asked to disrobe, Lucas bent over and unlaced and removed both his black shoes—polished, Martha noted, to a military shine. Another concession to Rani, perhaps. He lined them up neatly beside his chair, loosened his tie, unbuttoned his jacket and looked expectantly at Martha.

Sensing a way of easing the tension that was so obviously inhibiting him, Martha said: 'Let's go back to semantics for a moment, Lucas. I want to explore a bit more about what you might have meant when you said *this kind of psychology*. You mentioned the mind—which is a complicated concept in itself, as much about the gut as the brain and central nervous system. So you might be surprised to know where the word *psychology* comes from. Do you happen to know?'

Lucas smiled broadly for the first time since the session began. To him, this felt like a welcome transition from the uncertain and vaguely threatening world of psychotherapy to the safe and solid terrain of semantics. This ancient operator—his initial impression of Martha—had managed to hit on his favourite thing! He'd sometimes wished he'd done more formal study of linguistics and philosophy instead of engineering, though he wasn't sure how you'd earn a buck from it. It was a good hobby, though.

'Actually, I've never thought about it,' he said. 'Which is surprising in itself. But now you ask . . . well, *ology* is obviously *the study of*, just like cosmology or physiology or cardiology. Psyche? Ancient Greek origin . . . Wasn't Psyche the goddess of the soul? Something like that. Married to Eros, maybe?'

'You're spot on, Lucas. The Greeks used *psyche*—the word, not the goddess—to stand for what we might call life, or even spirit. The noun came from the verb *to breathe*—they thought the breath was the soul.'

Lucas looked at Martha in admiration. 'So that makes psychology the study of the soul,' he said, his rate of speech slowing appreciably. 'Which seems a bit weird, doesn't it? The soul? Ha! Funny that I'd never connected old Psyche with the way we talk about the psyche, or psychology . . . that's happened to a lot of words that came to us from ancient Greece.' Now he was on *really* solid ground. 'Cynic, for instance. Today's cynics are a far cry from the Cynics of ancient Greece. Respectable philosophers, back then. Ever studied the Cynics? Diogenes and those guys?'

'I have, as a matter of fact,' Martha said, surprised by Lucas's knowledge in an area she assumed was far removed from the world of IT. 'I once had my heart set on a career as a philosopher myself, back in the day. But my exam results said otherwise. Anyway, that's enough personal history.'

'No—I'm really interested. Please go on.'

'We're here for your story, Lucas, not mine. Tell me a bit more about your idea of the soul. You thought the link with psychology was a bit, um . . . weird, I think you said?'

'Well, yeah. I mean—the *soul*? Aren't we straying into the realm of theology? Or maybe that's about gods, not souls. But I mean, who talks about souls anymore?'

'Doesn't everyone? Think about it. We talk about throwing ourselves into things, heart and soul, don't we? Or about someone lacking soul? We talk about old souls. Soul music. A city with no soul. We even talk about soulmates. You might have explored that idea with Rani, no?'

'All just figures of speech, surely. But I get your point. A useful metaphor. The important thing is what we *mean* by what we say—as I keep trying to tell Rani.'

Lucas could hardly believe his luck. He had been almost paralysed with anxiety by the prospect of having to bare his . . . soul? Well, open his mind, anyway. Yet here he was, in the midst of a semantics tutorial with a woman who really knew her stuff—even if getting him to take his shoes off seemed highly irregular. Still, it seemed to be working. He did feel more relaxed, less . . . laced up, perhaps.

'And heart? You'd be happy about heart as a metaphor, too, wouldn't you? Not that energetic organ pumping away madly in your chest, but the seat of the emotions. Sick at heart. The leaping heart. The wounded heart. Remember how a moment ago I said, without consciously thinking about it, that I had my heart set on being a philosopher? We thank someone from the bottom of our heart, but that's nothing to do with physiology. What about the idea of giving your heart to someone—Rani, perhaps? At least in the beginning? You weren't talking about carving it out and handing it to her on a platter, were you.'

Lucas nodded. He was no longer quite so excited. The mention of giving his heart to Rani had sent a shock through him. That's exactly what he had done. Those were precisely the words he'd used. Barely four years ago.

Martha watched his shoulders droop, his face sag, and his eyes half close.

'I'd like you to say whatever you'd like to say about the heart, Lucas. That's why we're here. Hearts. Souls. Minds. This is Metaphor Central. Notice I even let you get away with Rani's *roadmap*, though I daresay there was no road involved, and no map, either.'

Lucas wondered if he would ever be able to tell Martha what was really weighing on his mind. Or was it on his heart?

Martha wondered the same thing.

FIVE

CONSTANCIA WAS ALREADY SEATED AND WAITING AT Pendolino when Rob arrived for their impromptu lunch. Climbing the stairs from the Strand Arcade, heavy-hearted, he saw her before she saw him. He'd always savoured the sight of her when she didn't know she was being observed, and he'd recently admitted to himself that part of this pleasure came from feeling that he was at a safe distance. Regardless of how bitterly they fought, or how often one or other of them might reach the point of certainty that their relationship was doomed, Rob never failed to register how beautiful she was. It was not just her voluptuous body or her lustrous long black hair, her dark eyes or her flamboyant way of dressing—today, a black silk shirt generously unbuttoned, tight blue jeans tucked into red boots, with a bright red belt and big brass buckle. He had once believed—was even now wishing he could still believe—that she was not just beautiful to look at, but a beautiful *person* as well.

A beautiful *person*? That was an assessment Martha would have struggled to endorse, based on her brief encounters with

Constancia. Martha found her constant flippancy amusing in small doses, but suspected it was a light concealment of a sarcastic and cynical disposition. Constancia's narcissism was obvious, even to Rob, though Martha thought it so extreme that it amounted to a personality disorder. Even the name Constancia—no abbreviations permitted—seemed to strike a jarring note, as though the woman's entire way of life showed contempt for the name her staunchly Catholic Brazilian parents had bestowed on her.

Rob was not as blind to Constancia's flagrant attempts at manipulation as he knew Martha feared he was. He was finally beginning to see their relationship as a folie à deux. He knew he was complicit in their mad dance, and yet he couldn't quite bring himself to let go of the last remaining fragment of his dream of some kind of life with Constancia. He had to admit there was no longer any joy to be found here, yet there was still plenty of excitement, and not all of it destructive.

Rob had always been grateful for Martha's patience when he had needed to vent his frustrations about his relationship—his fury at Constancia's various deceptions; his anguish over her shameless claims of dalliances with other men; her breathtaking self-centredness. There had been many occasions when he had been on the verge of calling it off, even rehearsing his farewell speech. But then, with impeccable timing, Constancia would overwhelm him with passion blended with remorse, and Rob would be pulled back from the brink. At such times, he wanted to believe her when she said how much she needed him.

Though he was currently staying in Constancia's ultra-contemporary apartment in Cammeray, with stunning views over the tranquil waters of Middle Harbour, he only ever did this in short bursts. Neither of them had settled to the idea of living together, and Rob only felt really at home in his own place—an older-style apartment in a quiet, leafy Lane Cove street. Constancia, having once seen it and mocked its 'dowdiness', had subsequently refused even to visit, let alone spend the night there.

Rob had often felt more like her boyfriend than her partner. Of late, there were times when he didn't even feel like her boyfriend. He recalled Martha's reference to the narcissist's need for worshippers, and in his most despairing, self-doubting moments he was tempted to describe his role in Constancia's life as no more than a drop-in worshipper, rather than lover. And he suspected that during the periods when he retreated, wounded, to his own apartment, other worshippers might be equally welcome to drop in.

Early on, when he was casting around for ways to stabilise their relationship, he had briefly entertained the idea of proposing marriage. Yet he knew Constancia was implacably opposed to the very idea of marriage—for herself or anyone else. She had once told Rob that when a close friend had confided in her that she was about to announce her engagement, Constancia had reacted with such hostility that the friend immediately left the lunch they had been having together and later refused to invite Constancia to the wedding. She reported such things to Rob with no apparent hesitation, as if it should be taken for granted that she was not the marrying kind and couldn't really imagine what it must be like to be that kind of woman. Or man.

Despite their conservative religious convictions, Constancia's own parents had divorced dramatically and acrimoniously when she was a teenager, and she often described that as the roughest passage of her life. But Rob was sure her resistance to marriage ran much deeper than that. It was rooted in a profound—Rob would hesitate to say 'neurotic'—need for freedom and independence, even within her most intimate relationships. She feared having her wings clipped by the demands of *any* convention or *any* institution, most particularly the institution of marriage.

She had also made it very clear to Rob that she never wanted children—partly, she insisted, because of her commitment to her academic career. She taught creative arts and was contemplating a doctorate in gender studies. Her reading in that field was a source of endless debate and occasional outright war between her and Rob, whom she regarded as not only an unreconstructed male supremacist, but also an unreconstructible one. The greatest mystery, according to Constancia, was how she could love a man like Rob, let alone lust after him. Sometimes she declared that lust was all she felt; this made her more comfortable with the whole arrangement, she said, but frequently caused her to question what would happen when that tank ran dry.

Rob had always assumed he would become a father one day, though he'd never have described it as a burning desire. It had merely seemed an attractive probability. At fifty years of age, though, that probability seemed to be diminishing. Earlier in his relationship with Constancia, he had tried to imagine what it might be like to co-parent with her. That was a tough one. Their kids would certainly know where they stood with her—she had a black-and-white view of most things—but how would she cope with a daughter who wanted to wear pink?

⁓

Pendolino was their favourite haunt for dinner, but midweek lunches together were rare. Since this was Constancia's idea, Rob assumed there was an agenda that couldn't wait.

As he approached the table where Constancia was busy on her phone, she caught sight of him and smiled. She stood and greeted him with a powerful hug and a wet kiss on the lips. She was almost exactly his height, and her long, strong hugs often made Rob feel as if they were prize-fighters in a clinch.

'Why the misery face?' Constancia asked, pulling one of her own trademark silly expressions.

'Misery? Me? No, I'm brimming with my usual irrepressible optimism. You?'

'Overflowing with the joy of. Cold wet day. Blowing a gale. Traffic's horrendous. Parking's an expensive nightmare. The maître d' couldn't find my booking. What's not to love?'

'You drove?'

'Yes, I drove, reckless eco-vandal that I am. On the other hand, I'm taking the rest of the day off, so I'm actually halfway home. And there's a bus strike on, in case you hadn't noticed, so it was car or cab. Not much difference.'

A waiter came and hovered at their table. Constancia smiled warmly at him and picked up the menu.

Rob said: 'I need to get back for a three o'clock client. You mentioned you were taking the rest of the day off. What brought that on?'

Constancia ignored the question and scanned the menu.

'I'll have the cannelloni,' she said to the waiter, 'and he'll have the mushroom and leek pie. Better get that moving. My friend is in rather a hurry. We'll think about drinks.'

'I won't be drinking,' Rob said, no longer irritated by Constancia's habit of ordering for both of them. 'My client wouldn't appreciate the smell of alcohol on my breath.'

'Is this your Belle from Belrose?'

'No comment. It was indiscreet of me ever to have mentioned her. But she does tend to focus on things like grog breath. And unpolished shoes.'

'Hmm. Well, I won't be drinking either. Not before my appointment.'

Rob paused in the act of pulling a bread roll apart. 'What's the appointment?'

'Oh, didn't I mention it? I'm booked in to have my tubes tied tomorrow morning, but the gynaecologist wants to see me this afternoon. Just to run through the procedure, I think, or maybe just for the pleasure of seeing me again before he does the deed. I won't look very pretty tomorrow.'

'Getting your tubes tied? *Tomorrow?* We've never discussed this. Why now, all of a sudden?'

'Discussed it? Why on earth would we have discussed it? I'm perfectly happy to tell you I'm doing it—actually, I thought I had mentioned it, but if you can't remember, then maybe I didn't. Anyway, it's not a *we* thing, it's a *me* thing. They're my tubes.'

'But, Constancia, surely . . .' Even as Rob began to frame the question, he knew it was pointless: Constancia would regard decisions about her body as the business of no one but herself.

As if to confirm this, Constancia ostentatiously ignored Rob and looked around the restaurant. She examined her nails. She picked up her phone and scrolled through some messages. Rob stared at her, feeling a strange mixture of annoyance and concern. A tubal ligation was not a small thing, surely. Not inconsequential. Not without its risks, like any surgery. Plus a general anaesthetic.

The food arrived and there was a pause while they each took a few mouthfuls. Still troubled, Rob couldn't resist returning to his question: 'Really, Constancia, isn't that the kind of thing we should at least have talked about?'

'Should? *Should?* Don't *should* me, Robin. We didn't talk about the termination, so why talk about this? Anyway, we're talking about it now, aren't we?'

Rob's face was ashen.

'Dear God, that *is* a misery face. What's wrong now?'

'The termination? What termination? Am I living in a parallel universe of some kind? We certainly never talked about a termination, Constancia, I can assure you of that.'

'Oh, that was ages ago. A couple of months, at least. I remember now. We were not even sleeping together at the time of the great discovery. You were in one of your *I-need-some-space* phases. So I was giving you space. Respecting your wishes. Sensitive, huh? I thought I might have mentioned it at the time, but obviously I didn't, judging by the stricken look on that gorgeous face of yours. You could play Lear with a face like that. Ever thought of an acting career? Could be more fun than you seem to get out of what you do now.'

'Constancia, rewind. *Fast.*'

'What, back to the bus strike? I dunno. I think it might have been about wages and conditions.'

'Please. Be serious for a moment. You were pregnant, but you didn't think to mention it to me? And then you had a medical termination? I was the father, presumably. Wasn't I entitled to be consulted?'

'The *father*! God, what a drama queen! The father of what? I didn't even see it on the way out. Bit of blood. Bit of cramping—quite nasty, but no worse than my periods when I was a teenager. The *father*? You must really be desperate for a bit of identity, you poor bugger, if you want to claim *that* as fatherhood.'

'But—'

'But *nothing*, you idiot. We have discussed countless times the fact that I will never, never, never have a child. Never. Have I not been clear about that, right from the start?'

'Yes, but—'

'I may have misled you about some things, Robin, but not that. You want fatherhood, you'll have to look for it somewhere else. Not this uterus. Yes, it was a shock discovering I'd botched my contraception, but it was a simple thing to correct. Do you imagine we should have had a heavy scene about it? Weeping and wailing and gnashing of teeth? No way, mate. Nothing could have been more straightforward. I'll tell you exactly what happened, okay? Listen carefully.'

Constancia planted her elbows on the table, rested her chin in her hands, fixed her gaze on Rob and said, very slowly, in the metallic monotone of an android: 'Forgot to take the pill. Got pregnant. Went to the doctor. Got hold of the magic tablet. Got rid of the thing. Life went on. And on. And on.' She sat back in her chair and gave a defiant toss of her head. 'Now, did any of that make a jot of difference to you?'

'How could it? I didn't even know.'

'Precisely. You were *needing some space*, remember? I shouldn't have mentioned it even now. File that one under careless slips. And not *Freudian* slips, thank you, Mr Psychologist.'

'Anyway, this thing tomorrow—When? Where? Do you want me to come with you? Or pick you up afterwards?'

'It's a procedure, Robin. Very straightforward. But, yes, I am counting on you to drive me to and from. After those awful things you said last night, I wasn't sure if you were planning to stay at my place tonight or not. Either way, I need you to get me to North Shore Private at the ungodly hour of seven in the morning.'

'Yes, of course. And it will be easiest if I stay at your place tonight. We'll need to be away by six-thirty. Look, Constancia, I admit I'm still feeling a bit shaken up by last night's melt-down . . . and now this. But I'll have to go in a minute. Do you want coffee?'

'Do I want coffee? When have I ever *not* wanted coffee? I *live* on coffee, in case you've forgotten.'

'So, do you want to discuss last night? I kind of assumed that might be why we were having lunch. I don't like even repeating the words, but you did say you thought you wanted to bring our relationship to an end.'

'Well, that was probably true last night, considering the way you were behaving. It's true a lot of the time. Don't you feel that yourself? The sense of an ending?'

Rob shrugged.

'But not tonight, Robin. Tonight, let's have wild and carefree preoperative fun. No deep-and-meaningfuls, okay? No tragic faces. Look, I've even bought something new to wear.' Constancia held up a shopping bag. 'Bit of silk. Bit of satin. Bit of lace. But I won't spoil the surprise. Think of it as a celebration—a happy send-off to my useless eggs. Or maybe just another horizontal festival of reconciliation. We're becoming good at those, aren't we? For such a serious fellow, you've managed to learn rather a lot from me about simply having fun. Right? Credit where it's due?'

All these mad games. All this brinkmanship. Why was he so reluctant to act? To seize the opportunity to bring this thing to an end, once and for all? Rob's mind was clear about what needed to happen; it was only the insistent yearnings of his loins that restrained him from standing up right now and walking away. He wanted—needed—to be free of her . . . *and* he always wanted one more night in her bed, though he despised himself for it.

'So what's going to happen?' he asked.

'Oh, the drivers will return to work, probably tomorrow, and the whole thing will blow over. The government will offer them less than they want. Same old, same old.'

'Very funny. I meant, what's going to happen to *us*? I mean, after your . . . procedure is out of the way. We really need to talk about—'

'Oh, I just remembered,' Constancia said briskly, as if Rob hadn't spoken. 'There *is* something else I wanted to tell you. My lovely gynae has promised to slip me some testosterone to keep my precious libido on the boil.'

Rob said nothing. He was beginning to despise Constancia as much as himself.

SIX

THE ORTONS WERE SITTING AT OPPOSITE ENDS OF THEIR dining table, glaring at each other. The evening was closing in and, though the room had become dark, neither of them felt like turning on a light.

'I thought this was meant to be a productive experience,' Bill said. 'Isn't that what you told me—*a productive experience*? Well, insulting that woman, humiliating me and crashing the car didn't feel very productive. And what was all that rubbish about me needing to speak up for myself, after you'd got me to agree to let you do all the talking? Or am I missing something?'

'Well, obviously I didn't mean to crash the car, and I had to say *something* about you—about us—to make it seem realistic.'

'Abby, you need to put me in the picture. The full story, please. You told me we were doing this for a good friend. Who is this *good friend*? And you told me Martha Elliott deserved it. Why? We don't even know her! How do we know what she *deserves*? I just felt embarrassed by the whole thing. I couldn't wait to get out of there. Talk to me, for God's sake.'

Abigail rose from her chair, and Bill flinched. But she was only heading for the kitchen.

'You're puzzled. Okay. I get that. More importantly, Martha Elliott is puzzled, which is exactly the way we want it. Today was just a shot across her bows. A teaser. You'll see. All will become clear. Be patient. To quote your favourite Australian prime minister, I'm going to do her slowly.'

Abigail filled the electric kettle and turned it on. 'Now . . . tea? Or would you prefer a drink?'

'I'd prefer an explanation.'

'I'm sure you would. But to paraphrase another former prime minister—*not* your favourite, this time—I will decide who can know what's going on, and the circumstances in which they can know it.'

'I'm sure you meant that to sound mysterious, Abby, but it comes across as a bit—what? Nasty? Malevolent? If you're so sure Martha did something she shouldn't have, I take it this is some sort of revenge project. Is that it?'

'Oh, revenge. Such an unpleasant word, Bill. And malevolent? Nasty? As you'll see, those are totally unfair charges. This is about justice, Bill. Pure and simple. It's about righting a wrong. A really, really serious wrong. And mysterious? Well, it suits my purposes to keep Martha—and you—in the dark for a little while longer. But let me assure you, dear heart, you're on the right side of the argument with this one.'

Bill looked across at his wife busying herself with the tea and, not for the first time, wished he didn't find her feistiness so disarming, so engaging, so . . . attractive. Whenever he dared question her motives or her judgement, as he increasingly found cause to do, her response was always the same: 'I'm worth it.' And Bill had generally found himself forced to agree, however grudgingly, with that assessment. He certainly didn't know anyone else as capable of surprising him as Abigail. He might sometimes have wished for a calmer life, but never for a less interesting one. Justice? He was certainly intrigued.

SEVEN

THIS WAS RUBY'S FIRST VISIT. THREE NEW CLIENTS IN ONE week, though the Ortons hardly yet qualified as clients. Martha had told Rob she wanted to cut back on her workload, but Sandrine had said this one sounded desperate.

As if to confirm that impression, Ruby cut the formalities short. She pulled an iPad out of her handbag, touched the screen, placed it on her lap, and started talking.

'So, I can tell you precisely why I'm here. You're probably not going to approve. Basically, it's a form of self-defence. I want to find out what the hell goes on between a counsellor and a client. Or maybe revenge is closer to the mark. I want us—you and me—to share the kind of secrets my husband now shares with this woman he sees every week. His counsellor, I mean. Well, he insists on calling her his *therapist*, as though that's a cut above. It's been almost a year, and the longer it goes on the more shut out I feel.'

Ruby touched her iPad screen again and looked up, but not at Martha. She had chosen to sit on a couch against the wall, well

41

away from Martha's chair, rather than on one of the closer chairs clients usually chose. Martha watched and waited.

'In the very beginning, I had no idea it was even happening. We used to have lunch together once a week. Mostly Wednesdays— we work quite close to each other in the city—but then things changed and I finally twigged to the fact that he was never available on Wednesdays. Too busy. A meeting, a lunch with a client—my husband's a lawyer—something always got in the way. I was irritated, because it had been such a pleasant ritual, but then I just let it drop and we even stopped looking for other days when we might both be free for lunch.

'So, eventually he tells me he's been seeing this therapist at lunchtime on Wednesdays for the previous six months. Six months! Felt he couldn't tell me because he thought I'd handle it badly. Well, I certainly handled being kept in the dark badly. I flipped, basically. I mean, I don't know how I might have reacted if he'd been upfront with me. Maybe I would have wanted to know why he felt the need to see someone. Yes, I would *definitely* have wanted to know that. I mean you don't watch your partner go off to the doctor without asking what the problem is. Not if you're in a halfway decent relationship, especially a marriage. But no, this was a deep, dark secret right from the off.'

When Ruby paused again to draw breath, Martha held up her hand and said: 'Ruby, I don't usually encourage my clients to read from notes. Is there something on that screen you'd like to show me?'

'Oh, sorry. This is my flow chart.' She held the iPad up to show Martha. On the screen was a series of interlocking rectangles, circles, arrows, question marks and large asterisks. There were very few words, none of them legible from where Martha sat.

'I see. You find that helpful to gather your thoughts, Ruby?'

'It's how I think. I think in flow charts. It's, like, my prompter. Are you okay with that?'

'Of course. Please go on.'

Ruby almost smiled through tight lips. She was a short, slim, neat woman, mid-thirties, dressed in a black business suit and stilettos that looked Italian to Martha, though fashion labels were far from her field of expertise. A blue silk scarf tightly knotted at her neck. Short brown hair beautifully styled and streaked. She looked to Martha like a highly organised, perpetually tense woman who expected everything—even a husband—to go according to plan.

'So, where was I?'

'You were explaining how you discovered your husband had been seeing a therapist for some time before he told you about it.'

'Right. So, once I knew it was happening, I'd say stupid things like, *I hope it goes well today*, or, *I hope you enjoy your session*, and he'd go, *It's not meant to be enjoyable*. Then, in the evening, I'd ask how it went and he'd go, *Fine*. Really helpful. Occasionally, I'd ask him straight out, *Will you tell me why you started going?* Or even, *Can you tell me what you talked about today?* Nothing. *Nothing*. I have no idea why he started going. Basically no idea what he talks about. It's private, he says. Personal. *Personal!* I thought that was the sort of stuff married couples talked about with each other. I mean, I'm not a trained psychologist like you, but I love this man—at least, I think I still do—*of course* I do—and I'd like to be able to be a bit sympathetic about whatever's bugging him.'

'I guess you'd expect him to mention anything he thought you might be able to help him with?'

'Exactly. Maybe there's something I can change about myself. Maybe I can try a bit harder. I'm not perfect. Never said I was perfect. I know I'm a cracked pot—we all are, aren't we?—but

I'm not a crackpot. But if I'm going to do better, I'd like to know how. I'm an engineer, for God's sake—give me a plan! Give me a blueprint! Do I talk too much? Or not enough? Who knows?'

Ruby glanced at her flow chart.

'Oh yeah: lockdown. So, it was even worse in lockdown. We were both working from home—no kids, yet, thankfully. My friends with kids say it was sheer hell, juggling work and home-schooling. Talk about stress! So anyway, he switched to phone sessions with Madam. We share a study at home, so I had to clear out while he talked to her. Even through the closed door, I could hear the sound of his voice. Totally unnatural. Totally unlike his normal way of speaking. When he'd finished, I accused him of doing a Leonard Cohen impression—all gravelly and tragic. As if he'd switched into a different gear for the benefit of this therapist. As if he wanted to make it sound as if he was this really sad, wounded guy. *And that's not Vincent!*'

Ruby took a deep breath, and Martha took the opportunity to interject.

'None of us is just one thing, Ruby. People often behave differently with different people.'

'Yeah, whatever. Anyway, after that, I cleared right out—went for a long walk—whenever he was scheduled to talk to her.'

Though the flow of words had been torrential, there was something about Ruby's delivery that seemed strangely clipped. Staccato. Her hands were clasped tightly together, resting on her knees, her arms almost straight. Martha was reminded of a whippet she once owned. It was not hard to imagine Ruby holding her own in a roomful of men and taking no nonsense from any of them.

The wounds she was describing struck Martha as coming straight from an engineer's nightmare—being thrust into a situation over which she had no control whatsoever, and which she felt unable even to comprehend.

'I basically assume if it's something he doesn't want to discuss with me, it must be *about* me. Or us. So I've asked him that, too. Straight up. *Is this about us? Or me? Am I such a difficult person to live with that you need weekly counselling to cope?* When I ask him that sort of stuff, he looks at me as if I'm a child and says things like, *It's not all about you, you know.* As if I've got tickets on myself. So does that mean it's something he wants to keep *hidden* from me? Like, is he in some kind of trouble he can't share with me? What kind of a marriage would it be if that was true? You can see how a person can end up going round in circles.'

Ruby stopped talking and her arms briefly relaxed. It was as if she'd put her weapon down to reload.

After a pause, Martha said: 'You feel as if Vincent should be able to talk to you about anything that *isn't* directly connected to you or your relationship? Is that it?'

'Yeah, pretty much. But not only that—what about all the stuff that *is* connected to me and our relationship? Here's the thing: I know it doesn't have to be like this. Compared to one of my girlfriends . . . chalk and cheese. Totally. She's seeing a psychologist, and she says it has brought her and her partner closer together, because she likes to talk to him about what went on in the sessions. Not everything, necessarily, but the stuff she thinks would be helpful for him to know about. Stuff that's going on in her head that concerns him and their relationship. There's none of that with us, though.'

'So has Vincent never complained about something you do or don't do? Never given you a hint of something that might be bugging him?'

'Only once. He said he thought I was too close to one of the men at work, and he was having trouble dealing with that. That was total bullshit. Total. I work in an all-male office. All my colleagues are guys. It's a blokey profession, engineering, and I'm naturally closer to some of them than others. Like this particular guy, Jerry. Sure, I do have personal conversations with him about his wife and kids, stuff like that. Life in general, sometimes, I guess. But nothing remotely *off*. He's more a colleague than a friend. But he is a friend, too. We have lunch together some days. But he's not the kind of friend I could discuss this problem with—no way. That's strictly girl talk.'

'*Strictly* girl talk?'

'Sure. There are some things you can only talk to other women about.'

'You mean things you wouldn't even talk to Vincent about?'

'Yeah. Maybe. I see where you're going with that. Anyway, Vincent has this theory that there's no such thing as a purely platonic relationship between a man and a woman. He thinks there's always something else going on, even if it's unspoken. I find that basically pretty offensive—sleazy, actually—when I think of Jerry and some of the other men I work with, to say nothing of some of my girlfriends' rather dishy partners. Vincent says the only safe male friend for a woman is a gay man. Never says the same thing about men. Maybe his shrink—oh, sorry, therapist, whatever—is a lesbian. I never thought of that. Shouldn't matter, should it? Anyway, I told Jerry he was my honorary gay friend. I had to explain what I meant. Luckily he was amused.'

'I'm pleased you got a laugh out of it. The story you're telling me sounds rather grim. As if it's really clouding your whole relationship with Vincent. Is that right?'

'I have tried to lighten it up a bit. Sometimes, over dinner on a Wednesday night, I might say something like, *Have they found a cure yet?* Or maybe, *Any blinding insights today?*'

'And how does Vincent respond to comments like that? Do you think he finds them funny, too?'

'Oh, no. Not at all. We're not allowed to poke fun at any of this. In fact, he's become pretty humourless all round. He used to be chirpier. Maybe the poor guy is depressed. I never thought of that. I don't think he's taking any pills for it, though. But maybe that's another little secret of his. Fuck. Oh. Sorry about the language.'

Ruby dropped her head for a moment, then raised her chin as if she were determined to stay strong.

'There's no need to apologise, Ruby,' Martha said. 'You can say whatever you like in here. And that's really the whole point about sessions like this. Or sessions like Vincent is having. If you can't feel free to be totally open with me, then we wouldn't get far, would we?'

Ruby looked sceptical. 'Yeah, I guess,' she said. 'But how long can this go on? I've heard of people who stick at it for years and years. Like, what's that about? I sometimes think this woman— Joanne, apparently—might have become his best friend. Practically his soulmate. Funny, isn't it, when he's the one who says a relationship between a man and a woman can never be entirely platonic. Still, I never ask him how he *feels* about his so-called therapist. No, that's not true—I did ask him once if he likes her and he said he does, or he wouldn't be able to work with her. So goodness knows how long this will go on. In fact, another one of my little Wednesday jokes is to say, *Well, that was visit number thirty-two*—I just make up a number—*so this obviously isn't working yet.*'

'I do understand that you're feeling frustrated about this, Ruby. And I can assure you there's no such thing as a typical length of time for a counselling relationship to last. Some people do stay with it for years. Some people come and go a bit. Some people feel they can clear up a difficulty in a few sessions. But I can see it's hard to be on the sidelines. You'd like a progress report occasionally. I get that.'

'Exactly. I mean, if it wasn't working, you'd think he'd stop. But on the other hand, he might keep hoping it *will* work—like sticking with a boring movie in the hope it will eventually suck you in. So even if it's not working *yet*, you can't stop. Maybe it is working at one level. How would I know? But working in what way? It's certainly not working for *me*.'

'Can you say a bit more about that, Ruby? About how it's not working *for you*? I mean, it's Vincent who thinks he needs help. The critical thing is that it's working for *him*, surely?'

There was a long pause. Ruby looked briefly at Martha, hesitated, and finally said: 'It would be working for me if I knew what the fuck was going on, or even if I felt it was bringing Vincent and me closer together. And as for working for *him*, I'd just like to see a bit of evidence that he's better off than he was before he started seeing this woman.'

'And you can't see that? I mean, there's no sign of Vincent being more relaxed? Or more confident in himself? More comfortable in his own skin? Or . . . or perhaps different in some way?'

'Ha. Different? Yeah. Different alright. More uptight. More secretive. Haven't you been listening? More sure of himself, maybe, but not in a good way.'

'I get the downside for you, Ruby. I really do. I'm just wondering if you can imagine an upside for Vincent.'

Ruby frowned. 'Upside for Vincent? Dangerous territory, Martha.'

'How do you mean?'

'An upside for Vincent is what I fear most.'

'Tell me more about that?'

'Look, I don't really get this about men, but I do know that . . . well, for some men, if you're not getting enough sex, or what you're getting isn't good enough, a certain kind of guy might go and pay someone for it.'

'But you're not suggesting that's the case with Vincent.'

'Of course I'm not. It had better bloody well not be! But what if he's paying this woman to be his no-holds-barred best friend instead of me?'

'Plenty of married people have "best friends" as well, you know.'

'Yeah. Best mates. Whatever. I'm talking about . . . I don't know. I guess I'm talking about intimacy. I'd hate—I'd really *hate*—to think there was more intimacy between Vincent and Madam than between Vincent and me. But there might be. It might be just like that. If it wasn't, you might think that eventually he'd sit me down and tell me the whole story. Maybe crack a bottle of champers to celebrate the end of the process—*I'm cured!* That type of thing. Maybe even to mark a milestone—*Today we had a real breakthrough!* But deep, deep, *deep* down I know that's not going to happen.'

'Tell me a bit more about what you mean by intimacy, Ruby.'

'Ha. Very astute, Martha. You don't miss a trick, do you? Only last week, Vincent told me it's not possible to have the kind of intimacy I want. What do you make of that?'

'What did *you* make of it? Can you recall the context?'

'Oh, the context! You're sounding like Vincent. The context. What do you think the context might have been? I was complaining, of course. What else? About our *lack* of intimacy. About how he had more intimacy with his therapist than with me. That was the context. Same old, same old.'

'So what kind of intimacy do you think Vincent was referring to?'

'Not sex, if that's what you're thinking. No, he thinks I'm too full on. Wanting to know everything about each other. Wanting to be completely transparent. "Naked", he calls it.'

'Well, intimacy is a very subjective thing, Ruby.'

'Yeah, I get that. I sometimes think about Diana—remember her? The princess? She'd be an old woman by now, if she'd survived. I remember watching this doco on TV where she said she felt as if there was a third person in her marriage to Charles. Well, there's most definitely a third person in our marriage, I can tell you that. I feel it when we go to bed. I feel it when we go to a movie or a concert. I wonder: *What's he going to tell* her *about this?*'

'You feel inhibited?'

'It's like treading on eggshells. On Tuesdays and Wednesday mornings, I keep hoping I won't do or say anything that might upset him enough to tell on me when he's in his session. Or even something to go down on the list of examples of why . . . oh, sorry, I forgot. It's not all about me, is it? Anyway, he has his session at lunchtime on Wednesdays, and then I feel grumpy on Wednesday nights and Thursday mornings—we never make love on Wednesdays, so it's really only plain sailing from Thursday night to Monday night. So, yeah, three people in our marriage. Maybe you'll be number four, Martha. Ha ha. How do you feel about that? The fourth wheel. Hey, maybe that's not such a crazy idea. Maybe you'll stabilise things for me. That'd be awesome.'

Ruby's attempt at a laugh came out as more of a choked cough.

'I once made the mistake of referring to his mental illness,' she went on. 'Never again. Furious reaction to that. He goes, *What mental illness?* I said, *Well, if you're going to see a therapist there must be something there that needs fixing.* He almost exploded. *No way! You don't understand the first thing about it,* blah, blah, blah. Which is perfectly true. I don't. Which is the whole point! But you know what? I think maybe *I've* got a mental illness. Sometimes I'm out of control with worry about what's happening with Vincent and me. Literally. Out of control. Out of my mind.'

Without even the warning of a tremble in her voice, Ruby suddenly burst into tears. After sobbing for some minutes, she dabbed her eyes, blew her nose noisily, and gazed imploringly at Martha.

'I'm hopeless, aren't I? Even I can see that. If I was Vincent, I think I'd need to see a counsellor too. Therapist. Whatever. But it wasn't like this before. I never felt deceived before. Kept in the dark. Now I do, all the time. Why is it such a big fucking secret? Tell me that. Go on, tell me. You're in the business.'

Martha got up from her chair and walked across the room to where Ruby was sitting on the sofa. Their time was almost up, but she decided to extend the session a little. She sat beside Ruby and asked her if she would like Martha to hold her hand for a moment. Ruby nodded and tried to smile, and Martha took one of Ruby's hands in both of her own and said, very quietly, 'In this office, no one is hopeless. No one. Certainly not you, Ruby. Most certainly not you. And, yes, you're right—we are all cracked pots, but that's just like saying we're all human.'

The two women sat in silence for a moment until Martha said, 'Now, Ruby, I want you to do something for me. Just slip your shoes off and lean back and we'll do a bit of deep breathing together. We won't talk for a few minutes. We'll just sit here and relax together.'

Ruby, still sniffling, did as Martha suggested. 'So maybe I'm your very first hopeless client,' she said with a watery grin.

After a few minutes, Martha returned to her customary chair. Ruby picked up her shoes and bag and moved to one of the closer chairs.

'Now I'd like us to wrap up our session with a bit of fun,' Martha said. 'Let's talk about anyone's marriage but yours. Maybe start with your parents' marriage. Are they both still alive? Uh-huh. Still together? Okay, tell me a bit about them. How would you rate their marriage? Like doing a stress test on a building or a bridge. Go on—give them a score out of ten. Be as ruthless as you like. Then we might do the same for Vincent's parents. Or that girlfriend you mentioned.'

After Ruby had left, Martha fell to wondering, as she often did, how many of her own clients were trying to use her as a supportive, sympathetic friend rather than a therapist. The Freudians called it *transference* but, whatever you called it, it was a danger that always lurked. And Martha knew that some of her non-counselling techniques—like those foot massages that Rob liked to mock—might well increase the risk. Blur the boundaries. She also wondered how open her own clients were with their partner, if they had one. Did their time with Martha encourage or inhibit greater intimacy at home? She knew some people found it far easier to expose their innermost thoughts to a therapist than to a sexual partner. And not everyone wanted the kind of intimacy Ruby yearned for. Martha herself had also yearned for it—ached for it—but had never found it in a partner, except once, fleetingly.

EIGHT

DRIVING TO BALMORAL BEACH IN RESPONSE TO SAMANTHA'S urgent request to meet for lunch, Martha experienced a familiar surge of complex emotions as she started the steep descent from the Spit Road ridge straight down Awaba Street. The bay lay sparkling below her, a Manly ferry still pitching as it completed its crossing of the heads, assorted boats bobbing at anchor and, even in the winter sunshine, a few swimmers, canoeists and paddleboarders enjoying the water.

Balmoral, for Martha, evoked nostalgia for the endless summers of childhood. The fond remembrance of falling in love for the very first time on this very sand. But also the lingering pain of recalling how a divorce had been agreed to as she and her soon-to-be ex-husband strolled along the promenade, looking just like any other couple taking the evening air.

Martha had learned to swim here, in the baths fenced off from the open water. She had learned to paddle a canoe, in the days when they could be rented from an office on the wharf. She had learned to flirt here. She had an album full of old family photos that captured every phase of her childhood and adolescence, and many of them were taken right here on Balmoral Beach. In the beginning it had been a bus trip from Willoughby, though there was a photo in a family album of Martha as a baby in her mother's arms on a Balmoral tram. Then a car ride, when hers became the last family in their street to acquire a car. Then a series of far hairier rides in friends' cars and, just once, on the back of her boyfriend's motor scooter.

She ached for Balmoral if she stayed away too long, and sometimes she came here at the end of a working day, just to sit on a bench facing the bay, perhaps to eat fish and chips and admire the Bathers' Pavilion—the background to many of those old family photos, and captured even now in a Robert Billington photograph hanging on the wall of her living room.

She had asked herself many times why she didn't live here, and never had a satisfactory answer—except, perhaps, that Balmoral had always been a place to *come to*, to escape to, over and over again, with that perpetual sense of rediscovery. Would the magic fade if she lived here? Yes, she thought. Roseville was a far more sensible—to say nothing of affordable—place to live if you worked in Chatswood.

Even in winter, parking was an issue at Balmoral. She eventually found a spot up a side street and walked the few minutes to the restaurant where Sam would be waiting, together with the man she had described in her phone call as her 'prospect'. Martha knew all too well what 'prospect' meant, and part of her was wishing that such a meeting could take place anywhere but here. The relaxed, romantic overtones seemed inappropriate, somehow. She had to concede that Balmoral might have held as many happy memories for Sam as it did for Martha, though probably not yet as many poignant ones, but couldn't imagine which kind of memory might later be evoked by this meeting.

The restaurant where they were meeting hadn't existed when Martha was a young regular at Balmoral. Then, one day, it rose from the scrub at the southern end of the beach and had become a favourite meeting spot for Martha and Sam, long after Sam had left home and begun to demonstrate her entrepreneurial flair as an interior designer. At such lavish places, it was always Sam's shout. Already wealthier than her mother would ever be, and very beautiful, but still alone: Martha struggled to understand that about her daughter.

She knew where to look for Sam and there she was, seated at her favourite table with a view of the beach and beyond. Opposite her, with his back to Martha, sat the prospect. A healthy head of wavy dark hair was all Martha could observe at first glance.

Sam jumped up and smiled as her mother approached. Martha couldn't help it—she was dazzled by her daughter's appearance whenever they met after even a few weeks apart. Sam's beauty was a continuing source of wonderment to Martha. She regarded herself as terminally plain, and wondered how she came to have a daughter like this, though people often said that Sam had her mother's eyes. Almost a foot taller than Martha, Sam always stood out in a crowd.

Martha was also grateful for a daughter who still smiled at her with such obvious warmth, when several of Martha's friends—to say nothing of some of her clients—were effectively estranged from their adult offspring, or were struggling to adapt to a hurtful coolness whenever they met.

'Mum, I want you to meet Darren. Darren, this is my lovely mum, Martha.'

Darren rose from his chair, looked Martha directly in the eye and shook her hand firmly. So far, so good, thought Martha. Her place was set beside Darren. She noticed that the fourth chair had been removed, and Sam was seated centrally opposite her two guests. An advantage of this was that Darren wouldn't feel as if he were facing an inquisition, but it meant Martha wouldn't have the opportunity to study him as closely as she would have liked. Still, he seemed handsome enough, in a craggy kind of way—in fact, quite reminiscent of one of Sam's boyfriends from long ago. Darren looked quite a bit younger than Sam, too; closer to thirty than forty, Martha thought.

They scanned the menu. Sam summoned a waiter and the rituals were all impeccably observed, as if this were a perfectly normal social occasion.

When the entrees arrived and drinks were poured, Sam said: 'So, Darren. Tell us a bit about yourself. Work? Sport? You look pretty fit, pretty healthy, if you don't mind me saying so.'

Darren put his knife and fork down, and turned to Martha. 'Samantha doesn't muck around, does she?' he said. 'Straight to the point. I like that.'

'So?' Sam persisted.

'Nothing spectacular. I'm an accountant. Didn't have the personality to become an auditor. That's a joke in my line of business—I have quite a fund of accountant jokes . . .'

Sam, who was watching him intently, allowed herself a polite smile. 'And?' she said, not to be deflected. A true daughter of her mother.

'What else can I tell you? I play a bit of touch footy. I surf in summer. But there's not that much time for sport, what with the job and the kids.'

'The kids?'

'Two girls. Real sweeties, the both of them.'

Martha, shameless pedant, flinched inwardly at 'the both of them', then reminded herself that a grasp of grammar and syntax wasn't a hereditary trait.

'How old? Do you have any pictures?' Sam needed more information—as much information as she could reasonably extract from this man. Martha knew she was becoming desperate.

'Oh, five and seven. Young. Yeah, I've got a few pictures on my phone. Take a look.'

Sam grabbed the phone and began scrolling through the pictures with obvious eagerness. Martha thought this rather unseemly, though she knew exactly what Sam would be looking for. Signs of good genes. Good skin. Good hair. Good build. Straight shoulders. Bright eyes. Nice smiles. Good teeth—the seven-year-old's second teeth would be in, and Sam would be assessing them for whiteness, straightness, size.

Darren was one thing, but the products of his sperm were a far better source of evidence for Sam. This was unusual for her—to be looking at the actual offspring of a prospect. Previously, she'd had only the prospect himself to go on.

'Thanks, Darren. They're really lovely,' Sam said, and Martha was relieved to hear that small courtesy. She didn't ask to look at the pictures, and Sam didn't offer to show them to her.

Sam handed the phone back to Darren. 'And how does your wife feel about you . . . you know, donating?'

'Oh, I did it a few times before we got together. When I was a student.'

'And do you keep in touch with any of those children? Or their mothers?'

'One, yes—occasionally. The mother, really. Not the kid. Just over the phone. The others, no. Although I think the law might have changed and the kids are allowed to track me down later if they want to. Why would they, though?'

'Biological parent. Could be interesting to a young person growing up. Depends what their parents tell them. How do *you* feel about all that?'

'Well, I'm not into diblings parties, like one of my mates is. But I'd be cool with meeting up, if they really wanted to. Yeah.'

'*Diblings* parties?' Martha couldn't resist asking.

'Yeah. So one of my mates goes to this picnic once a year where all the kids conceived from his donations get together. Donor siblings. Diblings. I don't even know if it's a real word. The mothers are all there with the kids. And he turns up. Hero of the hour, type of thing. Superdad. I think those must be mothers who've been very upfront with their kids from when they were old enough to understand. I'm not sure I'd be up for that. One at a time, maybe, but not all at the same picnic.'

'You said you keep in touch with one, but not the others. How many others?'

'I think there are three. Yeah, four all up. You can never be completely sure. Why?'

'Just wondered. No issues with your fertility, then.'

'Nah, not yet, anyway.' Darren laughed in a way that Martha thought slightly unpleasant. Was he bragging? It reminded her of Simon, her ex-husband, being so proud of producing a baby with his much-younger second wife, a woman Sam had never been able to warm to. The lack of an appropriate age gap between her and Sam possibly made her seem more like a very remote stepsister, Martha assumed. She'd never really explored that with Sam. Simon's new life was a topic Sam seemed unwilling to discuss.

'So, Darren, are you ready to go through this again? And your wife . . . I'd need to be sure your wife was totally on board. Is she do you think?'

'Well, I haven't told her yet about us having this meeting. I didn't realise your mum—Martha—would be here too. But Julie will be cool with it. Why not? It's nothing to do with her, really, is it?'

'Well, I guess she'd want to know if you were planning to play any role in the child's life, wouldn't she?'

'Probably, yeah. Although Julie's pretty cool with everything, if you know what I mean.'

'But let's be clear, Darren. I'll be raising this child on my own. I won't be calling on you for anything at all. Not for financial support, obviously, but not for any other kind of support either. If we go ahead, no one must ever know I found you on that Facebook page, okay? If the child wants to know who you are later on, that would be up to him or her . . . and you, I guess. We'd have to look into the legalities of all that. But there'd be no birthday cards, please. No little bulletins from me about school progress. This is pure biology, okay?'

Darren turned to Martha. 'Your daughter could teach my Julie a thing or two about getting to the point.'

'Dessert, anyone?' Sam was picking up the menu again and switching back into social mode. Martha was both impressed and appalled. She wasn't sure she enjoyed seeing her warm, gorgeous, creative daughter being so ruthlessly clinical. But she was pleased to be included in the assessment process. She supposed it was a bit like Sam inviting a boyfriend home for dinner to get the once-over from her mother. A tiny bit like that.

They had arrived in three cars, all parked in different areas. Darren left first. He shook hands with Martha. She watched Sam walk with him towards his car. Bursts of laughter reached her, Darren's deep and rather attractive, Martha had to admit, and Sam's achingly familiar. They moved out of sight and earshot and Martha waited, distracting herself by watching some toddlers playing with buckets and spades in the wet sand. Some things never change, she thought, then remembered why she was there, and decided that some things change very profoundly indeed.

Sam eventually returned, walking briskly and looking flushed.

'I'll walk you to your car, Mum,' she said.

'No, I think I'd like to take a moment to stroll along the beach. I don't have a client until four. Want to join me?'

'I really should go. I have an inspection and quote in Glebe at—'

'Will a fertility clinic be involved in all this? I mean, I'm sorry. It's none of my business—except that I *will* be the grandmother. But I have the feeling Darren's passed the test. Am I right?'

'Probably. There's a young Italian guy who's offering a good price—and some very nice pictures—but I'm not sure how we'd get his sperm into the country.'

'But wouldn't the fertility clinic look into all that? Aren't you going to get Darren to . . . I don't really know how these things work. But I'm thinking doctors—reproductive experts. I mean, it's not a do-it-yourself thing, is it?'

'Relax, Mum. Yes, I think Darren's sperm might be the go. What did you think yourself? I mean, don't worry about the way he handles his knife and fork; we're strictly into genetics here. Would the blend of Darren and Samantha produce a positive result? You didn't see his kids. They were gorgeous. The older one had teeth to die for, and they both had really lovely skin. So does Darren, as you saw. Their hair was finer than Darren's—that must be from Julie.'

'And so is your skin lovely and so is your hair finer than Darren's. But really, Sam, surely this isn't only about teeth and skin. You make it sound as if you're choosing new tiles or taps for your bathroom.'

'Actually, Mum, it is a bit like that, to be honest. What else do I have to go on? I'm not going to spend a month with his kids to see how smart and well adjusted they are. All I want is healthy sperm. Teeth and skin and hair are not bad indicators.'

'Oh, Sam. I don't really know what to say. I don't know what you want me to say. If you had been showing Darren off to me as a potential suitor—Lord, where did that word come from?—I think I'd be urging caution. But, well, I'm not so good at assessing sperm quality. Even if you gave me a microscope, I wouldn't know what to look for. Strong swimmers?'

Martha sighed deeply and gazed across the water. Another ferry was ploughing through the swell as it passed North Head on its way to Manly Cove. Martha wanted to be on it. *Seven miles from Sydney and a thousand miles from care*, the old Manly ferry posters used to promise.

She looked back into the earnest face of her daughter. 'I do think Darren is a much nicer-looking man than that rather weedy specimen you rolled out a few months ago,' she said. 'But, Sam, look . . . I'm out of my depth. Really I am. I know you're committed to having this child. We won't go over that again. I know this is the sort of backdoor way you want to manage it. I know you're a strong woman. But I still worry about . . . I'm not sure what I'm worried about. I suppose I am worried about you embarking on motherhood all by yourself. Well, not *all* by yourself. You'll have old Grandma here for back-up. But I do worry about you trying to manage all this outside the system.'

'Oh, Mum. *Outside the system!* The counsellor who offers foot massages and meditation on the side? Outside the system? Believe it or not, the system isn't very interested in eggs as old as mine. But don't worry about it. I've read up on the subject. There's some very good material available online. I know exactly how to approach it. And maybe, just maybe, I know what I'm doing. Is that a possibility, Mum?'

Martha frowned and nodded her head almost imperceptibly.

In response, Sam placed her hand on her mother's arm. 'How about I spare you the details? If I turn up on your doorstep with a bottle of French champagne, you'll know what it's about. I won't be toasting Dad's next baby, if there is one. Okay?'

'Of course it's okay. I think the Balmoral air affects me. I can't help thinking of us coming here when you were a littlie. You were so cute and vulnerable. And I still think you're cute and vulnerable.'

'You're pretty cute and vulnerable yourself, for an old bird.'

They embraced, and held each other for a moment or two longer than usual, both resolving, for their different reasons, never to mention Darren's name again.

Martha watched Sam walk away. Then she slipped off her shoes and socks, rolled up the legs of her pants and began to walk along the sand. It was low tide and there was more seaweed lying about than usual. It looked and smelled like decay, and some of it was sharp and prickly against her bare feet. Unpleasant. Martha couldn't recall that smell from previous visits. She kept walking towards the island that was not, in fact, an island but a tiny promontory. Everyone called it 'the island', though. People call things what they want them to be, Martha thought.

She walked closer to the water's edge, and let some of the gentle waves wash over her feet. Ruby and Lucas floated into her mind, and she wondered if they ever walked on a beach with their partners. Was there a special beach in their history, too? She never really asked any of her clients about their attachments to place. It could be a serious omission. If anyone wanted to understand *her*, they'd need to get her to talk about the significance of this place in her life. It would be a long conversation.

A number of seagulls were lined up on the wall of the promenade, watching a young couple eat hot chips from a paper cup. Eventually, the young man threw a chip in their direction and several of them swooped at once and squabbled over the spoils. There's enough to go around, Martha thought, if only we could learn to be patient. Enough love. Sam had more than enough to bestow on a fatherless child—Martha knew that. It wouldn't be grandmotherless, though, and she found that a consoling thought.

The young couple threw the rest of their chips to the gulls, and Martha returned to her car.

NINE

AFTER FORTY YEARS AS A THERAPIST, MARTHA RARELY experienced anything remotely like trepidation as she waited for a client's arrival. But she had to admit that the looming appointment with Abigail and Bill Orton did not arouse the normal rather pleasant tingle of anticipation. She had half-expected either an apology or a cancellation, but had received neither.

When the knock came, it was more like a tentative tap, and when she opened the door, the Ortons were looking remarkably meek, possibly even contrite. She ushered them in.

It occurred to Martha that getting them to remove their shoes would be one way of slowing another attempt at a premature exit, but she decided she'd bide her time.

'Please sit down. Before we say anything else, I'd like to begin today with some simple breathing exercises. Is that okay?'

The Ortons seemed in no mood to object to anything, and Martha ran them through a few deep-breathing routines with no apparent resistance from either of them. Abigail had her eyes closed, and seemed to be fully in the moment. Bill was simply doing what he was told, and it occurred to Martha that it might well be the story of his life.

'Now,' Martha said, when the breathing was done and she had allowed a suitable pause, 'there's no point in avoiding the events of last week. I see you've recovered. No physical injuries, Abigail?'

'Oh, no. I'm sure it sounded far worse than it was. Although the other driver was a very unpleasant fellow, and I was glad of Bill's support.'

Abigail turned a loving gaze on Bill, and Martha had another of those unsettling flashes of doubt that any of this was authentic. Too strident last time. Too gooey, this time.

'So let's make a fresh start, shall we? I wondered if you might like to try a little exercise that clients often find rather helpful. I'm going to ask each of you to represent the other's point of view. It's a simple device, really. But it can be particularly helpful if one partner is feeling a bit misunderstood, or not being listened to attentively by the other. Sometimes, that discipline of putting yourself in the other person's shoes can be quite clarifying for both parties.'

Abigail stiffened visibly. Bill leaned forward as if he might indeed be willing to give this a go. He glanced at his wife in a way Martha had trouble interpreting. She thought it could be a warning of some kind. But a warning about what? To keep her cool, perhaps? To stick to some agreement to go along with whatever Martha suggested?

Unsmiling, Abigail said, 'I'm happy to play that little game if you really want to. If Bill wants to. He can go first.' She spoke without looking at either Martha or Bill.

'Okay, Bill?' Martha continued. 'Then why don't we go back to last week and think about why you came here in the first place? Or, if you like, why you decided to come back again today. But give me Abigail's version. Tell me, as if you really *were* Abigail, why you think you're here.'

'What—do you mean you want me to talk as if I'm actually Abby?'

'Precisely. It's just a discipline, Bill—a way of trying to imagine Abigail's view of the world.'

Bill laughed, then stopped abruptly in response to a stern look from Abigail.

Seizing the moment, Martha said, 'Just before you start, Bill, would you feel like saying something about your laughter just then?'

'Laughter? I, er . . . well, I just thought it sounded a bit like a child's game, and I reacted childishly. Will that do?'

'Do?'

'I mean, will that do as an explanation of why I laughed? I only laughed, for God's sake. It's not a big deal, is it?'

'It might be or it might not be. I just noticed that you laughed at the moment when I asked you to imagine Abigail's view of the world. Can you replay the moment in your mind?'

'Well, yeah, I guess anyone who tried to imagine Abby's view of—'

Abigail interrupted him: 'Bill, stop! Now! Okay? And you, Martha Elliott, stop playing God, will you? Deep-breathing exercises, little role-reversal games, as if this is Management 101 or something. What next? Colouring-in books? A bit of cooperative play with some Lego? Manipulation, pure and simple. I *hate* the high-handed attitude that's implied. It's like a virus that finally infects *all* you so-called therapists. You think you know what's best for everyone. You offer your opinions as if they're holy writ. You *interpret* whatever we say as if *your* interpretation is the only valid one. It's such a superior fucking attitude. Medical specialists are bad enough, but they're not half as bad as you lot. You think you *know*, don't you? You think you've got some secret code the rest of us can't crack. The inside story. *Bullshit!*'

Martha sat calmly through this diatribe. She'd heard far worse in her time. Unsurprisingly, clients often became aggressive when they were feeling vulnerable. It crossed her mind that, if only Abigail knew what Martha really thought, she'd be astonished by the extent of their agreement with each other. Except for her mockery of the breathing exercises and role reversal, Abigail was expressing some of Martha's own deepest reservations about the profession she'd dedicated her life to. She, too, was in despair about the superior attitude of many of her colleagues, as if they did, indeed, possess the keys to some dark inner sanctum where life's secrets were revealed only to them. She shared Abigail's scepticism about therapists who thought their theoretical framework was the only correct one, the only possible one. And yet, once again, she couldn't help wondering whether Abigail's outrage was real or confected.

She looked at Bill. His mouth was hanging open in astonishment, and Martha wondered whether that, too, was authentic or contrived. She amused herself for a moment by imagining how Abigail might have reacted if Martha had indeed invited the Ortons to remove their shoes. She still believed it might have helped.

'So, Bill,' she said, 'are you ready to start? Maybe Abigail has given you some more material to work with.'

Again Bill laughed. Abigail shot him a look of undisguised fury. Martha raised her eyebrows involuntarily.

'Go ahead, Bill. I think we should proceed. I'll come back to Abigail's remarks a little later.'

'Spoken like God herself,' Abigail said, but there was no heat in it.

'Well,' Bill began, 'where should I start? I've sometimes felt that Bill was rather too acquiescent, and I thought we needed some help in sorting that out. Encouraging him to speak his mind a bit more. Be a bit more assertive. I sometimes feel—I'm speaking as if I'm Abby, remember—I sometimes feel as if I don't know where I stand with Bill. He's basically a nice guy; perhaps too nice for his own good. He tends to agree with me too easily, although he was a bit reluctant when I suggested coming here to see you. I'm pretty sceptical about therapists myself—I'm still speaking as if I'm Abby, remember—but I'd heard that you were pretty exceptional and so I thought it was time we gave this a try. I guess I'm hoping these sessions might bring out a side of Bill I know is there but haven't really seen for years.'

Bill glanced rather anxiously at Abigail, and then at Martha. 'How was that?' he asked.

'Well, only Abigail can answer that question, Bill. After all, you were trying to impersonate her. How did he go, Abigail? Did that sound like a recognisable version of you?'

'Oh sure, yes, whatever. But I'm not playing that stupid game. I don't deny there are stresses in our marriage, and I *would* like Bill to speak up for himself a bit more. Not just with me, but generally. I said that last time. Not that I really expect we'll make much progress. Bill was not quite right about that part. I hadn't heard you were exceptional. I'd just heard that you were less hopeless than some others. But we'll keep at it for a while, I guess. Something might turn up. Right, Bill?'

Bill nodded, like a man reluctant to risk saying another word.

'So, Abigail,' Martha said, 'now Bill has given us his version of your reasons for coming, how about you doing the same for him? Speaking as if you're Bill, now, why do *you* think you're both here?'

Abigail looked harried. She was practically wringing her hands. Again the question arose in Martha's mind: was she acting?

'Oh, alright. If I must. Let's see. If I were Bill, I think I'd say I was dragged along, completely against my better judgement, by my domineering wife who said there were some issues in our marriage that needed to be resolved by a professional. I didn't even know there were any issues, so that probably proves she was right— I mean, if she thought there were and I thought there weren't.'

Abigail looked at Bill.

'Okay, comrade? Sound like you?' Her voice was suddenly soft and solicitous.

Martha was not convinced by it, but Bill appeared to be. He looked at Martha and then took a tissue out of his pocket and began wiping his eyes. His tears, at least, seemed genuine.

Hi Gabs
Progress! Stage 2 wrapped. ME puzzled but not
ruffled. She's a tough one. I'll give u the gories
tonight. 10? Btw, I uttered the f-word. I cd practically
feel the thwack of Dad's strap across my butt. Ouch.
Abs xox

> *Don't remind me. Better make it 11, Abs. There's a*
> *bit of drinking going on here.*
> *Gabs xox*

TEN

'LISTEN TO THIS, DEAR. "HOPE YOU ARE SAFE AND DOING well." Isn't that kind? From a total stranger, too. Someone called Claudia Jones. Actually, Claudia emails me several times a week, though not as often as Sienna Brown or Michelle Diamond. I sometimes hear from little Sienna two or three times a day. This morning, for instance, she wrote to me asking if I would be interested in a brand-new website. Imagine! I also get quite a lot of these young women asking me if I'd received the email they shot across the other day. That's how they put it. *Shot across.* Very colloquial. Some of them are more polite—I get a lot of them *reaching out* to see if I would like help with my social media management. My *social media management*, Martha. I wonder who they think I am. Some are not so careful with their expression. I get "Hope you are doing great" quite a lot. I hate that. *Doing great.* I was a teacher once, a lifetime ago. If one of my pupils, or even one of the grandchildren, said that to me, there'd be some very explicit correction, I can tell you. Although, they're Americans, of course, the grandchildren . . .'

The client went into a brief reverie, and Martha was reluctant to interrupt. Then she was off again.

'Now, where was I? Oh, in the beginning of all this, I replied to some of them. I gently chided Brandy Silver *and* Crystal Taylor on their misuse of "great", and the missing "I" at the beginning of that sentence. Or non-sentence. I assured Jessica Bonde, Scarlett Collins and Shereen Khor that, no, I didn't want a brand-new website, and I thanked Violet Sparky and Dawn Avril for their interest in my social media management but explained that, as I wasn't on any social media, their assistance would be redundant. I even questioned Marry Baker about whether she might have wrongly placed that "r". Surely she must be Mary Barker? No parent would name a child "Marry". Or perhaps I'm out of date. You do hear some strange names. Some of my correspondents have *very* strange names—Samira Monica, for instance. Do you think she got her names round the wrong way? Or what about Merrit Bonway? I actually looked Bonway up in the phone book—yes, I still have a phone book—and there appears to be no such surname. I tracked down a Bonway auto repair shop via the internet—in California, I think it was—and there's a Bonway Investments, though I wasn't personally in the market for anything they appeared to be offering. Actually, I couldn't work out *what* they were offering.

'Anyway, I never heard back from any of those women—just a message from my email server saying my replies were undeliverable. I think of them as *young* women. It's those names. No one of my generation is called Brandy or Merrit. I also hear from the menfolk sometimes—Hosea Niles and Trinidad Ives are two names I remember—but their messages tend to be more long-winded and less polite. Is that a gender thing, do you think?'

Martha seized the opportunity created by her client's question to speak. 'Mrs McCrossin—'

'Oh, call me Hazel, please, dear. No one calls me Mrs McCrossin anymore—not even total strangers on the phone, or the receptionist at the doctor's. It's all *G'day, Hazel* these days. So, Hazel, please.'

The legs of her black tracksuit pants had ridden up, and Hazel pulled them back down over her socks. She was wearing a faded pink windcheater on top, over a grey sweater. Her hair was in need of a wash.

'Thanks, Hazel. I was only going to suggest that—'

'Oh, I know what you're going to suggest. You think I'm a crazy old woman who actually believes these are real people writing to me. No way. It's all computer-generated, Martha, I realise that. I didn't at first, I grant you, but when you get exactly the same message on the same day from three different names, you soon work it out. What I can't work out is, why me? Why do I get thirty or forty of these messages every single day? Someone told me it's because my email address appeared on the garden club website. Why we ever bothered having a website, I'll never know. Anyway, I'm talking too much. You say something, Martha. My son thinks I need your help. Bless him. He's in California, too, like that Bonway repair shop.'

Martha looked into Hazel's face and saw a sadness that seemed to have taken up permanent lodging, as if Hazel had adapted to it, absorbed it, and now made no attempt to conceal it. Her client information form said she was seventy-nine, but she looked and sounded older than that. Martha had sensed from the start that this was a woman diminished by social isolation and ravaged by loneliness. She was too smart, obviously, to have taken email spam seriously, but it suited her to pretend she did—or not even to pretend, but just to play with the idea that these were 'real' messages. If nothing else, perhaps they were a distraction that helped pass the time.

'Do you get much other email, Hazel? I mean, apart from all that computer-generated stuff? You mentioned your son. Does he keep in touch? What about the garden club?'

'Oh, the garden club disbanded last year. Too many members were dying. Too many funerals. Too sad. Anyway, I don't have a garden anymore, so I'd stopped going.'

'And your son?'

'My son? He's a real success story, Jason is. A fine man. Lovely American wife, two children—well, they're young adults now, and Americans, as I mentioned. He has a very big job in the film business. *Hollywood*, Martha! I can't say I'm exactly sure what he does. He's very busy, of course. But, yes, he rings me on my birthday and Christmas and that, and I told you he was the one who said I needed to talk to you. Well, not exactly. He said I needed to talk to *someone* . . . It was my GP who suggested . . .'

Hazel lapsed into silence, and Martha waited.

Eventually Hazel spoke again. 'You think reading all those silly emails and wondering about those silly names is a bit pathetic? So do I, Martha.'

Another long pause.

'I'm not stupid. I know full well that the endless messages from Sienna Brown don't mean a thing. They're not really addressed to me. She, he or it won't even accept a reply—I tested that, as I told you. But the thing is, I still like to receive them. I enjoy looking for the similarities and differences. The patterns, if any. I like criticising their poor grammar. I think I'd probably miss them if they dried up. Same with those leaflets I get in the letterbox from Australia Post. I know they don't actually come from the nice people in my local post office, but I like to think they do. I read them out of respect for those people. I like to think these things are personal, even though I know they're not.'

Martha nodded, smiled warmly at Hazel, and remained silent.

'I'm not exactly fooling myself. But I can see how it might look like that. I think it's harmless fun. Well, not exactly fun. But harmless. I do crosswords, too. They're harmless fun. Well, they're not much fun either, to be truthful, Martha. Better than jigsaws, though. But, see, I tell people I enjoy them. Why do I do that? Because I want them to believe . . . I don't know. Anyway, at least I don't tell people I read whatever Brandy Silver sends me. But I'm glad I've told you. This is really good—talking to . . . you know . . . someone.'

Martha nodded again, smiled again, and remained silent.

'The biggest lie I ever tell people, and I tell it all the time, is that I love living on my own. I tell them I really value my freedom and my independence. I tell them I can go out and meet people whenever I want to—which isn't strictly true, either, although there's a lovely woman on the Coles check-out who is up for a chat if they're not too busy—and then I can come home to my own little place, shut the door and feel peaceful and safe. Do you want to know the truth, though, Martha?'

'I think I can guess.'

'I bet you can. I don't feel peaceful and I don't feel safe. It's noisy, because I could only afford a place on the Pacific Highway. I have two locks on my front door, plus a security screen door, because I live on the ground floor and the front door of the block is open to the street. Bars on the windows, of course. Chatswood isn't what it used to be, is it? The neighbours in my block . . . well, *ruffians* would be unkind, but they are certainly rowdy, some of them. Rough diamonds, possibly. A few are really nice, though, and there's this one young man who says hello whenever we see each other. During the Covid lockdowns, he asked if he could do any shopping for me, which I really appreciated. I really did. Haven't seen him around so much since things opened up, though. Maybe he thinks I don't need any help now. But a chat would be nice, once in a while. That wouldn't occur to a young bloke, though, would it? Chatting to an old boiler like me, for no reason?'

Hazel fell silent. She looked at Martha and attempted a smile, but it faded before it could take hold.

'There you have it. The unvarnished truth. I *hate* living on my own. I'm so lonely, I—well, you know what I do. I devour email spam. I feel affection for all those stupid, non-existent Siennas and Brandys and Michelles and Crystals. Most of my real-life friends are gone—either dead or spirited away by their families, who thought they'd be better off in a retirement village or—get this—an aged-care facility. An *aged-care facility*. We don't call them nursing homes anymore. You probably knew that.'

'I did, Hazel. Yes. It probably does sound a bit less awful, though, doesn't it? Although "facility" does seem rather impersonal. Not very welcoming, perhaps. Is that what you think?'

'I'm too healthy—that's my problem. Eighty in a few months' time—way past the use-by date for pap smears, I can tell you. And most other things, too. If I could afford it, I'd move to one of those retirement villages myself. Just for the company. I feel so nervous where I live, I turn the TV on when I go out so I won't have that awful feeling of coming home to an empty flat. People call it an apartment—my son calls it an apartment, because that's the way he'd like to think I'm living—but it's so tiny, you should really only call it a flat. Or a unit. We used to call them home units. Remember that?'

'I do indeed,' Martha said. 'Look, Hazel, I think we've done enough talking for today. I have an idea. I wonder if you'd let me wrap up the session with a little foot massage. Would that be okay with you? I know it's not strictly part of your counselling session, but I'm quite experienced. People seem to enjoy it. It certainly can't do you any harm.'

'A foot massage? Never had one of those. Does it tickle?'

'I can promise it won't tickle. All it will do is relax you a bit, which I hope will be pleasant. Then we'll talk some more next week. Okay?'

Without another word being exchanged, Hazel took off her sneakers and socks, and pulled up the legs of her tracksuit pants.

'I'll try anything once,' she said.

ELEVEN

THE ORTONS' EVENING MEAL HAD BEEN EATEN IN SILENCE.
Abigail was still sitting at the dining table checking her messages.
Bill was cleaning up the kitchen.

Eventually, Bill said what he'd been wanting to say for hours:
'Game's up, Abby. You went too far.'

Abigail looked up from her laptop, eyebrows raised. 'You think?
Or maybe not far enough. She didn't seem rattled at all, did she?
She didn't even seem offended when I uttered the f-word. Which
I thought I carried off rather well, didn't you? I quite enjoyed
saying it.'

'She's a professional. I'm coming to think she might be a bloody
good one, too.'

'Steady, Eddie. Don't start wavering on me. I thought your
performance today was brilliant. Really. Quite brilliant. Right
down to the crumpled tissue at the end. That was a flourish
I hadn't anticipated. You're quite the thespian, Bill.'

'Believe it or not, I wasn't acting. But I wouldn't expect you
to understand that. Look, Abby, I need you to know something.

I agreed to do this for a friend of yours—friend unnamed, though I think I could make a pretty good guess. We're talking about the Dark Twin, aren't we?'

'Hang on, Bill. That's my sister you're talking about. I know how you feel about her. I wish it could be different between you two but I've learned to live with that. So, yes, okay, I'll tell you that much and no more. We are doing this for Gabby. Or, more precisely, for someone who's very close to Gabby. Someone who was very badly damaged by Martha Elliott, if you must know. Very badly damaged. So badly damaged that our Martha should have been struck off, or whatever they do for psychologists.'

'Listen, Abby, I'd never describe *you* as an angel of light, but that sister of yours really is a deeply malevolent creature. Really. Anything you can do, she can do darker. Yes, I know she's your twin sister. Yes, I know how close you say you are to her. I get it. But I'm not prepared to fight some vengeful battle for someone I've never met who happens to be a friend of the Dark Twin. That's all a bit too tenuous for my liking. Who is this alleged friend, for a start? She might be as prone to reckless exaggeration as the Dark Twin herself. She might be another one with a fervidly perverse imagination.'

'Don't say *vengeful*, Bill. This is all about justice, not revenge. Do I really need to spell it out again? Martha did the wrong thing, big-time. We're in the process of righting that wrong. As for being an angel of light . . . well, we're certainly on the side of the angels. I can say that with confidence. We're simply teaching Martha Elliott a lesson she needs to learn. A lesson she'll never forget. And until we've completed our little mission, you don't need to know any more than I've told you.'

'Really? So I'm to be treated like a child—again. *You don't need to know any more than I've told you, Bill.* Great. Well, I'd say Martha Elliott is not going to put up with being treated so badly for much longer. Where are we heading with this? Are you trying to provoke her to the point where she'll actually lose her temper? Is that it? Or just banish you from her consulting room, which seems far more likely.'

'Oh, she won't do that, Bill. Not our Martha. She's puzzled, and that's good. But we need to see this process through to the bitter end, and so does she. You watch.'

'Hmm. If you say so. But, really, Abby, don't you feel even a little bit ashamed, embarrassed, uncomfortable—*something*—about all this deception? A bit awkward, at least? When you shrieked at her this morning—'

'I raised my voice. I didn't shriek.'

'Alright. Raised your voice. Whatever. Don't you ever feel a bit as if this is the wrong thing to be doing? Telling such blatant lies?'

'Lies, Bill? I meant every word I said today about therapists. I meant every word I said last time about hypocrisy. And, dear heart, I hate to break it to you, but I meant every word I said about you, too.'

'Yeah, yeah. I don't mean the words, so much. I mean the whole pretence of it. We're being deceitful just by being there, regardless of what we say. Devious, at least. Now you tell me we're doing this to right some terrible wrong done to some friend of the Dark Twin. I mean, come on, Abby. It's absurd. We're not authentic clients.'

'Authentic? Oh, yes, my husband's favourite word. Anyway, who says we're not? I have a very serious, very authentic purpose—I'd even say a noble purpose, Bill—as you will soon discover. Anyway, just one more session to go. Hang in there. Believe me, we're doing the right thing.'

Bill scowled but said nothing.

'In the meantime,' Abigail said, 'here's something else to ponder. When it comes to authenticity, what about Ms Elliott herself?'

'How do you mean?'

'This morning. What was the natural way—the *authentic* way—for her to respond to my rather noisy little outburst?'

'Anger? Resentment? Indignation?'

'Dead right. Yet you saw for yourself: not a ripple. Cool as a cuke. Don't tell me that wasn't an act.'

'But she's a professional. She knows how to control her reactions. She *needs* to stay calm. It's her job.'

'To be inauthentic?'

'To be impassive. Professional.'

'I rest my case. Anyway, isn't impassive just another word for cowardly? Martha Elliott is a coward *and* a hypocrite. You'll see.'

⁓

Hi Gabs
Bill pushed me to admit you're 'the friend'. He knows
nothing else.
Abs xox

> *No worries. That will just confirm his dark opinion*
> *of me. Of us. Is he a bit dim? I've always wondered. If*
> *the roles were reversed Himself wd have twigged.*
> *Gabs xox*

Yep. No imagination.
Abs xox

TWELVE

'HEY, MARTHA.'

Lucas had established a pattern of weekly sessions and was becoming progressively more relaxed and open. He was even beginning to relax his dress code and his hair was noticeably longer. Several weeks into the process, he strode into Martha's office in a polo shirt, jeans and sneakers, sat down and, unbidden, removed his shoes.

'That's better,' he said. 'Let's scramble.'

'Hello, Lucas. Good to see you again. Shall we take a few deep breaths before we begin?'

Lucas complied, though Martha felt he had not yet quite seen the point of it.

'When we finished last time,' she said, 'you were asking me whether I thought most people who come to a therapist with a relationship issue are actually looking for a way out of the relationship. You mentioned that a psychiatrist's wife had told you that. Actually, I seem to recall she was a psychiatrist's *ex*-wife. Is that right?'

'Exactly. So . . . is that your experience? Do they?'

'I'm not trying to be evasive, Lucas, but I don't feel comfortable talking about *most clients* or what other clients might or might not want when they come to me. There's no doubt that some people come to me when it's really too late in the process of separation for me to be of much help. Some do come because they've decided to end a relationship and they want guidance about how to go about it in the least damaging way possible, particularly if kids are involved. But some are genuinely trying to find a way back to the closeness they once felt in the relationship. Or the sense of security. It can be any of the above.'

Lucas was looking out the window as Martha ran through the list of possibilities.

'So . . . *Lucas?*'

'Ah. Yes, well, the question isn't entirely theoretical, is it? I've decided I've been keeping something back that you probably ought to know if we're going to maximise the potential for a positive outcome from this process.'

'Well, you are getting to know me quite well, Lucas. There are no rules about what ought to be said or left unsaid. You are free to say whatever you want or need to say and to hold back anything you'd feel uncomfortable about telling me.'

'The truth is, Martha, I don't feel uncomfortable about telling you anything, and I wonder if that's an issue, concept-wise. You already know more about the state of my mind—heart, soul—than Rani does. A lot more. Probably a lot more than Rani wishes to know, to be honest. Is that a problem for you? It does feel like a bit of a problem for me.'

'It's certainly not a problem for me, Lucas. But let me ask you this. How much of what we have been discussing here do you feel like sharing with Rani?'

'Sharing with Rani? The lot. I *feel* like sharing the whole enchilada with her. I feel as if there'd be a real breakthrough in our relationship if I could speak to her as freely as I can speak to you. I'm sure we could strategise a beneficial way forward.'

'Yet you have said several times that you believe Rani is fully committed to the marriage. There doesn't seem to be a question about that. It might not be as close as you'd like. Not as . . . carnal was the word you used right back in the beginning. A lack of empathy, perhaps, but no lack of commitment—to you, the marriage, the child?'

'Oh, the child. No lack of commitment there, I can assure you of that. Centrepiece of her life's montage. D'you like that? *Montage.* Her word, not mine. But yes—her core value, motherhood. Even though she started warehousing the child in day care when he was only six months old. From the outside, you might think her *job* was the centrepiece of her life's montage. But we don't really talk about priorities anymore. What's the point? Your priorities can only be established by looking at what you *do.* The rest is not worth the hot air it's written on. Sorry—that's another little BJA expression. But really, Martha, isn't it a bit counterproductive trying to define values at the conceptual level? Surely our priorities reflect our values, regardless of what platitudes we might mouth. Just check the evidence, I say. Hours per day—that's the only basis for accurate assessment of our priorities, wouldn't you agree?'

Martha nodded noncommittally. It sounded as if Lucas was drifting in the direction of his beloved statistics again. 'You were saying you'd like to discuss our sessions with Rani more than you feel able to?'

'No, that's not quite right. Remember, me coming here was Matt's idea, not Rani's. When I told Rani, she was, like, right on board with it. Ace idea. To be honest, when something tricky comes up or I want to discuss something with her that she can't be bothered with, she just goes, "Why don't you talk to Martha about that? That's what you're paying her for. That sort of stuff is in her job specs, not mine."'

'That sort of stuff?'

'The sort of stuff you and I talk about all the time. Feelings. Interpretations. God, she hates interpretations—mine especially. *It is what it is*, she says. *Don't pretend it's something else.*'

'Lucas, you sounded as if you were feeling uncomfortable about something when we started this morning. Do you want to say any more about that?'

'Two things, to be honest. One easy, one hard. The easy one is I was just trying to say it's not that I can't talk to Rani about anything we discuss—it's that I can't get her to listen. I can talk all night if I want to, but she's settling the child, or reading stuff from work, or even watching TV. She'll look up and nod occasionally, or maybe smile in a vague way. But no connection. No engagement. No reaction. I'm background noise. Aural wallpaper. So what do you think I do in response to all that?'

'Stop talking, I imagine.'

'Right. Stop talking, Lucas, I say to myself. Stop making a fool of yourself. Speak when spoken to. But it's no way to live. It grinds me down. It discourages me. I *like* to talk. And, in the beginning, so did Rani. To be honest, I fell in love with her voice. Rich. Deep. Throaty. A bit on the husky side. I used to say I loved what she said *and* I loved the music of her voice. I called it her speech-music. She loved me saying that.'

'And now?'

'Her voice is still wonderful. The words not so much.'

'You said that was the easy thing you wanted to tell me. It doesn't sound as if you find it easy at all.'

'No. But it's easy to tell you. The hard thing isn't.'

'Remember: you don't *have* to tell me anything you're feeling uncomfortable about.'

Lucas took a deep breath then said: 'The child is not mine.'

Having finally uttered the words he had been waiting so long to say, Lucas removed his glasses and covered his face with his hands. Martha remained silent, scarcely breathing. Not wanting to distract him with any sound at all. Minutes passed. Lucas didn't move. Martha wondered if he was covering his face like a child hoping to become invisible. Or to hide his humiliation. Or to hide tears.

Eventually, he dropped his hands and looked straight into Martha's eyes. She couldn't recall ever having seen such a sad face on such a young man. She nodded and said nothing.

'As soon as Rani knew she was pregnant, she went looking for a father for the child, and found me. I was very willing to be found. I admit that. Eager, to be honest.'

'Eager to become the child's father?'

'Oh no. Not that. Never that. How could I have been? She didn't explain what she was up to. I had no idea she was pregnant when I met her. No, I was eager for the love of such a warm, wonderful woman. Such a stunning beauty. The kind of woman I had never been able to attract before. My girlfriends to that point—well, I'm not even sure you'd call them girlfriends—were all mousy little things compared with Rani. She positively glowed with beauty. Radiated warmth. From the moment we met, she was like an ever-flowing fountain of love. That was her rather poetic turn of phrase. Not mine. But apt. Oh yes. Very apt.'

'Remind me how you met?'

'Through a colleague. All set up—dare I use the word *arranged*?—though I didn't know that at the time. Rani's closest friend knew she was pregnant and asked her husband if he knew anyone who might be suitable for Rani to date. Didn't tell him why, naturally. The husband works at BJA. Different department from me, but we occasionally chatted to each other at Friday drinks and, this particular Friday, he tells me quite casually that there's this friend of his wife's he'd like me to meet. Works in IT. Was I interested? I was dismally single at the time, and so it all sounded pretty terrific to me, concept-wise.

'So, long story short, the four of us had dinner together and I'd never . . . well, I'd never had a woman appear so keen right from the get-go. Keen and, indeed, amorous. The other two left the dinner early on some pretext, and Rani and I . . . well, there you are. Sex the first night. I couldn't believe my luck. I didn't know the subtext, though. I thought I must have suddenly become irresistible, as if I'd drunk one of those love potions. Like in a fairy tale, or something. No such luck. It was all very calculated. I didn't finally cotton on until after the birth, though.'

'And the child's biological father?'

'A one-night stand, according to Rani, though I must say I doubt that. It's a convenient story, but he was Indian, like Rani, and he was in Sydney on a six-month secondment from the IT company he works for in Bangalore. My guess is they had many, many nights together. My guess is she thought it was heading for marriage and he never did. I imagine that, to him, she was just one of the collateral benefits of the secondment.'

'Lucas, this seems to be a very different version of events from the one you told me before. About how you'd met Rani at an offsite—her PowerPoint presentation—love at first slide. All that. Am I confused?'

'Not at all. I told you the official version—the famous offsite story. Now I've told you the inside story. The real one. And yes, we *were* at an offsite together. Her HR outfit was doing some consultancy work for BJA. But we were already in a relationship. Secret, though, at Rani's request. Engaged, in fact, with a wedding already planned.'

'Then why bother with what you described as the official story? You could have told me the true version in the first place.'

'I didn't know you. I didn't know if I could trust you. And the official version really is the *official* version.'

'Surely it doesn't make much difference either way.'

'Ah, you don't know Rani. Appearances are everything. She wanted the more romantic version to stand.'

'An offsite is more romantic than an introduction over dinner with friends?'

'Less calculated. Chance. Fate. Unexpected encounter. The opposite of *arranged*. There's a lot of Indian stuff—a lot of family stuff—Rani is trying to shed.'

Martha sensed that she was looking sceptical. She knew it was unprofessional, but she couldn't help herself.

'I'll tell you something else about Rani. Totally unsentimental. Passionate, sexy, intense as, when she chooses to turn it on. Romantic, yes, in the classical sense, but never sentimental. Meeting at an offsite is about as unsentimental as you can get, surely?'

'Are you trying to convince me or yourself, Lucas?' Martha asked this with as light a touch as she could manage.

'I'm just giving you the inside story to the best of my ability.'

'Go on, then. I interrupted you.'

'Surely the details don't matter. The essential point is that I was deceived. I was deceived on day one. I was deceived into Rani's bed. I was deceived into thinking she'd got pregnant on that very first night together, and I was deceived into thinking that . . . well, this is the worst part. I was deceived into thinking that she really loved me with all that steamy passion. That she was swept away by her feelings for me. When I look in the mirror, I know that could never have been true. When you look at me now, I'm sure you can't believe it either, even without knowing Rani the Magnificent.'

Another lapse into silence. Another pall of sadness descending. If he feels that way about himself when he looks in his bathroom mirror, Martha thought, I wonder if he can imagine how I feel when I look in mine.

'She told me she was two months pregnant on our wedding day, which happened almost exactly two months after our first night together. Talk about whirlwind. I was stunned, needless to say, but also overjoyed, flattered, all those things. Naturally, I wondered why she hadn't told me right from the beginning, but later I realised it was because she wanted us to be legally married first. She might have thought I'd do a runner if we weren't married—which I never would have done. Rani was my prize! My trophy! Why would I ever have left her, baby or no baby?'

'Go on, Lucas.'

'Well, it all fell into place when it dawned on me that the allegedly dramatic premature birth was not premature at all. The child's birth stats were consistent with a full-term baby. I eventually calculated that she must have been at least twelve weeks pregnant on our wedding day, not eight.'

'Lucas, our time is almost gone . . .'

'Okay. But, look, I admit I did have a few doubts about the truth of what Rani had been telling me. Especially when my mother started commenting that Rani was looking too big for such an early stage in her pregnancy, unless she was having twins, which had never been mooted. At the birth, I took one look at the child, and realised it was one hundred per cent Indian. I was not entirely shattered, to be honest, because it was now perfectly obvious that our amazing instant conception on that first night was a fabrication. I confronted Rani with the threat of a DNA test and she told me the story of the infamous one-night stand. Even if it was a six-month stand, what difference does it make?'

Lucas began putting his shoes back on.

'And then there was the name. She was absolutely set on Felix, once she discovered it was a boy. I went along with that. After I heard about lover boy, I became suspicious and did a bit of research. It was easy enough to track down a Bangalore IT guy who'd worked in Sydney for six months. Not too many guys called Felix. Felix Kumar. I haven't bothered telling Rani I know who he is. He's right out of the picture, as far as I know.'

'It's an upsetting story, Lucas. I'm sorry.'

Lucas shrugged and tried to smile. After a very long pause, he said: 'I'll tell you what I would really like to happen, Martha. I would like Rani to love me the way she once pretended to. Or, to be truthful, even to pretend that she does. She can be pretty convincing. I'd be willing to be convinced all over again.'

THIRTEEN

MARTHA GENERALLY SUCCEEDED IN KEEPING HER OWN
awkward tale of concealed paternity out of her head, but then
something like Lucas's story would bring it back to the surface.
She would have strenuously denied any suggestion that she was
repressing it; it was simply a secret she had thought it wise to keep
safely locked away.

Except from one person—Giles Dubois—and the way things
turned out with Giles, Martha had long ago concluded that it had
been a mistake to divulge her secret to him. But that had been one of
those moments—she'd seen the same thing happen to clients—when
there's a rush of such affection for someone, a surge of such deep
trust, that we experience an overwhelming desire to surrender to
that person; to hold nothing back; to achieve the complete intimacy
we believe will come from complete transparency . . . and Martha
thought she had found that person in Giles.

She had never thought that way about Simon, the high-school
sweetheart she had married. Though they hadn't attended the same
high school, they met one day at the train station, when they were

both fifteen, and arranged to meet every morning and afternoon thereafter. There was no flirting—they were both too serious for that. But there was lots of soulful eye contact and occasional brushing together of hands. They started dating when they were sixteen, and finally got around to their first tentative kiss in the back of the bus on the way home from a swim at Balmoral Beach. Simon was Martha's one and only boyfriend.

Getting married had seemed inevitable. They had thought about doing it when they both turned twenty, but Simon's parents had insisted they wait until they had graduated. Martha's mother, a lifelong smoker, had finally succumbed to lung cancer the previous year, and her father, unable to cope, had gone missing. Given the circumstances, Martha had become very Simon-dependent.

Looking back, Martha's assessment was that it had been 'a reasonably okay marriage'. She and Simon had known each other for so long, there were no surprises. They had rubbed along reasonably amicably for about fourteen or fifteen of the twenty-three years they were married, though Martha had known Simon was cooling towards her long before he actually left. Martha herself had never contemplated leaving the marriage, since it had provided her with the stability she had craved, and she liked the thought of herself as a 'married woman'.

Having babies had been on the agenda right from the start—part of Martha's wish to establish a 'normal' family as quickly as possible. She'd had two traumatic miscarriages before she finally became pregnant with Samantha, and by then she was becoming reasonably philosophical about the whole idea of motherhood. It would happen or it wouldn't.

Simon, though, badly wanted a child. Martha hadn't imagined that a man could be so desperate to become a father and, after those two miscarriages, she had become anxious about the prospect of a third attempt. But, in response to Simon's urging, she took no precautions and waited for nature to take its course.

Which it did, in a rather unexpected way. Martha had attended a psychology conference in Adelaide, gone to bed with a cynical academic called Grant, become pregnant, and never told the truth about it to Simon—and certainly never to Grant, or Sam, or anyone else. Until Giles Dubois.

When she tried to explain her own reckless behaviour to herself—as she did on many occasions over the subsequent years—all Martha could honestly come up with were the conventional explanations. Alcohol. Hormones. Opportunity. Disappointment. More alcohol. Sadness. Frustration. Existential yearning. Forty years on, it still seemed unreal to her. The kind of thing that would never happen to someone like her. But back then, for a confused twenty-seven-year-old, all those factors had constituted a heady mixture. She had vaguely known Grant from a couple of previous conferences. Knew his reputation. Everyone did. He was the textbook likeable rogue, and Martha did like him, even though she privately thought him a somewhat ridiculous figure. But he was always fun to hang out with, and she had become quite attached to him, in a breezy, inconsequential way. He looked rather like an older version of Simon, which turned out to be convenient later—no one ever doubted that Sam was Simon's daughter. Martha didn't have Lucas's problem to contend with.

Over the years, her marriage to Simon became steadily drearier and more mundane. From Martha's point of view, it was companionable enough, but any hint of romance had well and truly gone. Which was fine, until it emerged that Simon was getting regular doses of romance elsewhere. Martha found herself curiously unmoved by his infidelities—possibly even relieved: there was no longer any need to pretend an affection she no longer felt. Her respect for Simon had long gone—he had turned out to be a devious operator in his financial services work—and so drifting apart had seemed like a natural process. She and Simon started sleeping in separate rooms but stayed together until Sam left school. They both turned forty-five that year.

Years later, Martha had looked back at some of her journal entries from that time and had been shocked to read her account of the split. By then she had seen plenty of people—clients and friends—going through the divorce process, and had always hoped she had been helpful to them. Supportive, at least. But when it came her turn to go through the wringer, she was simply over-whelmed by the brutal finality of it. The irrevocability. It had felt to Martha like the opposite of liberation. She had no sense of a new beginning—only an ending.

Although Martha had freely acknowledged to herself, and to some of her close friends, that the marriage had become hollow, to say the least, it was such an integral part of her sense of herself, she had never really tried to imagine the end of it. When it actually happened, she felt herself shaken to the core. Rattled. Unprepared. As she said to a colleague when the dust had settled: 'I'm sure I would have had something helpful to say to a client in that situation, but I had nothing helpful to say to myself.'

Reading that old journal, it seemed to Martha as if the worst part of the process had been dividing up their collection of books. As she wrote at the time: *Other things, household things, haven't really affected me at all—it was pretty obvious who'd take what. Even CDs weren't a problem, since our musical tastes are so different anyway. Those were his and these were mine. But the books . . . there was a collective quality about 'the books' that made me feel like a vandal, sorting and splitting them. It felt like emotional surgery. And yet, as we did it, I began to realise that the joy, or the inspiration, or the despair that each book might have evoked in either or both of us was unique to that book. And how many of them had we both read, anyway? When that process was complete, I felt the marriage was truly over, the divorce papers a mere formality.*

When the divorce and property settlement were done, Martha took twelve months leave from the practice she was working in at the time, organised the move from the family home to a small apartment, and devoted herself to Sam, who had just left school and was starting a fine arts degree and needing to make her own way in the world. As Sam became more engaged with her life as a student, she made it clear that she didn't need the day-to-day mothering Martha was imposing on her. Though initially hurt by this, Martha soon realised that she was probably overcompensating for her own lack of a mother at that stage of her life. She gradually regained her equilibrium, with the help of a no-nonsense therapist and a sympathetic GP, and went back to work. A year later, with Sam's strong encouragement, she started her own practice.

Simon didn't marry any of his paramours, which surprised Martha. She lost touch with him and he didn't even see much of Sam. And then, when he turned sixty and was apparently contemplating a change of pace, he wrote and told Martha he had moved to Cairns. Then he met and married a fortyish woman and had another daughter. 'That certainly will be a change of pace,' Martha remarked drily to Rob, when she heard the news.

FOURTEEN

THE DAY AFTER HER FIRST VISIT, HAZEL HAD BEEN ON THE
phone first thing, asking Sandrine for another appointment as
soon as possible. Sandrine had juggled things a bit and found a
slot for her at eleven.

At ten-thirty, Hazel entered the waiting room and sat in the
chair offered to her by Sandrine. She looked agitated, and frequently consulted her watch.

'Can I get you some tea or coffee?' Sandrine asked.

'What a kind soul you are,' Hazel said, 'but no thank you,
dear. I won't drink anything just now.' She looked around to
check there was no one else within earshot. 'The waterworks,
you know.'

At ten to eleven Martha's door opened and Hazel immediately
stood. But Martha was merely farewelling another client before
retreating to her office. Crestfallen, Hazel resumed her seat, and
Sandrine smiled at her reassuringly.

'Don't worry, Hazel,' she said. 'She's running on time.'

On the dot of eleven, Martha invited Hazel into her office.

Almost before she was seated, Hazel was tearing off her shoes and socks and pulling up her tracksuit pants.

'Good morning, Hazel. Is everything okay? Sandrine mentioned you were keen to see me again today. I'm pleased we were able to fit you in.'

Hazel had so far said nothing and now, as if miming, she pointed at her feet.

'Ah,' Martha said. 'You enjoyed the foot massage. You'd like to begin our session with another?'

'Yes, dear,' said Hazel. 'I mean, if that's all right with you. That was the first time anyone has actually touched me since goodness knows when. You don't realise how much you miss it until it happens.'

'I'm very happy to start that way, Hazel.'

Martha briefly busied herself with preparation and then pulled her chair closer to Hazel's. 'Before I make a start on your feet, let's do some deep breathing together. Just follow me. Okay?'

It was a few minutes before Hazel could allow herself to yield to the example of Martha's breathing rhythm, and then she closed her eyes and joined in. She knew it was a good thing to be doing, but it scarcely worked as a distraction from her urgent need to feel those hands on her tired and worn feet.

Eventually, Martha asked her just to breathe normally and began the massage. It felt to Hazel like an act of love.

Ten minutes, fifteen, passed in total silence, though Hazel shuddered once or twice, with the release of tension. When Martha was finished, she began to wrap Hazel's feet in a towel but Hazel asked her to continue holding her feet in her hands. 'Just for another minute or two, dear. There's something I need to tell you.'

There was another long silence, another shudder, and then Hazel began to speak, barely above a whisper.

'Do you know, Martha, when I moved into my flat, there was only one modification I had to make. I had the bath taken out. My friends said I was mad. My son said I was mad—he thought it would decrease the value of this grand apartment he imagines I live in. He'll get a shock if he ever comes to visit me. Anyway, it was a great palaver, with jackhammers and that, but I had to do it. I had a shower recess and a nice linen press built into the space and a bit of retiling, and now you wouldn't know a bath had ever been there. Quite an expensive operation. I was glad Clive wasn't still around to see the size of the bill. That's my late husband. I'm a widow, dear. Strictly speaking. It's a word I can hardly bring myself to say.'

Martha waited, but Hazel had drifted off into another of her reveries, possibly in memory of Clive.

'Hazel, would you like to talk a bit more about that bath? About having the bath removed? You said your friends thought you were mad. What did you tell them?'

'Oh! I told them a bath like that took up too much room and I needed more cupboard space. They thought a bath in a small flat was a great luxury, of course. Not me. I couldn't live with that bath. I tried for a while, but no.'

Martha continued gently massaging Hazel's feet, saying nothing.

'Do you keep secrets in here, dear? I mean, can I trust you?'

Martha smiled. 'Absolutely, Hazel. It's part of my professional commitment to you. Nothing you say here will ever be repeated. Sometimes I might talk to another psychologist if I need help sorting out a client's problems, but even when that happens no names or other personal details are ever mentioned. That's a faithful promise.'

Hazel looked into Martha's face, desperately needing to believe her.

'I'm eighty next birthday—I told you that yesterday—and I've never told a single soul what I'm going to tell you. Not even Clive. Especially not Clive.'

'Go on.'

'I used to love having my bath when I was a young girl. When I was a child, it was all baths, of course. Then I was old enough to have showers, but I still loved my bath, at least once a week. I used to look forward to it. It was my great self-indulgence. And then, when I was about fourteen, it all went very, very bad.'

Hazel fished in the pocket of her pants, pulled out a handkerchief and blew her nose noisily.

'Sorry, dear. Clive called that my trumpet solo.'

'Went bad in what way, Hazel?'

'It was my father, Martha. He started coming into the bathroom when he knew I was in the bath. There was no lock on the door—why would there be? At first, he'd perch on the toilet seat and just chat about nothing in particular—and I could tell he was looking at me in a way he shouldn't. But I loved him. I trusted him, of course. He was my father. You can probably guess what happened then. After a few weeks of just looking, he started touching me. All gentle, like, and murmuring stuff about what a special girl I was. At first, I was just embarrassed. Then . . .'

'Then?'

'It got worse. I just used to freeze up. I was scared out of my wits. I didn't know what to do. I couldn't say anything to Mum, and I couldn't talk to my little sister about anything like that; she was too young. And Dad was being so nice to me the rest of the time. Praising everything I did. Buying me treats. Taking me to movies I wanted to see, just him and me. Stuff that was too grown-up for my little sister. I thought I'd just stop having baths, but then he'd offer to run my bath for me. Big loud voice, so Mum could hear how lovely he was being . . .'

Another trumpet solo.

'It was the worst time of my life. I felt dirty, guilty, angry, sulky . . . I was rude to Mum and nasty to my little sister. I became a horrible person. I tried to ignore my father. I couldn't believe Mum didn't realise what he was up to. But I'm sure she didn't or she would have hit the roof.'

'How long did this last, Hazel?'

'Ah, so you do believe me, do you, dear? I was worried you might think it was a bit far-fetched. I mean, my own father. And it was such a long time ago. But you do believe me, don't you?'

'I do, Hazel. Of course I do.'

Then the tears came.

Eventually, through her sobs, Hazel said: 'I think it lasted about a year. Maybe a bit longer. Then I started going out with my friends, and I refused to be seen in public with my father. So he sort of backed off a bit. I think he might have started to get scared I'd say something to someone. I left home when I was seventeen to go to teachers' college in Sydney. That was the biggest relief of my life. I went home for holidays, but we never spoke about it, naturally. We never spoke much at all after that. I had come to hate him. I've wondered if he did the same thing to my little sister, but I could never ask her, of course. What would I have said? She's dead now, anyway. We were never close. I regret that.'

More tears.

'Wrong. Bad. Stupid. Too weak to stand up for myself. Letting a thing like that become a habit. Oh, but I paid a big price. I grew up feeling dirty. Ashamed. Wouldn't have a bar of boys. All through college. Frigid. Nothing till Clive, and I was twenty-four when I met him. And I haven't had a bath since I was about sixteen.

Never once. Strictly showers only. I still feel sick at the *sight* of a bath.'

Martha gripped Hazel's feet more firmly. 'Oh, Hazel.'

Martha was not unaccustomed to this kind of revelation. She was saddened, but no longer surprised, by the number of elderly women who came to her, possibly raising some other issue entirely before eventually opening up about incidents of sexual abuse in childhood or adolescence.

She reassured Hazel that she had done nothing wrong, that it was utterly and entirely her father's offence, and that, yes, her secret was safe with Martha.

'Bless you, dear,' was all Hazel could say, and the session concluded in silence, with Martha still holding Hazel's feet firmly in her hands.

As Hazel was putting her shoes and socks back on, she said: 'I knew I did nothing wrong. But that didn't seem to help. Anyway, I've told you now. I promise I won't phone again tomorrow and hassle that poor woman. I think I'll be fine, dear. Thank you.'

'I'm pleased you feel that way, Hazel, but I would like to see you at least one more time. We'll do some breathing. I'll do your feet again. We'll just take it quietly and see if there's anything else you'd like to talk about. Okay? Anything at all.'

'Well, yes. We'll see. But I would like another . . . you know. The feet.'

FIFTEEN

AS THEY USUALLY DID AFTER THEY HAD EACH SEEN THEIR last client on a Friday, Martha and Rob were having a debrief over a glass of wine. It was their habit to raise any client issues they were grappling with, but also to ruminate more generally. The Life and Times Hour, Rob called these sessions. A recently recurring theme for Martha had been her concern about Sam's determination to undertake a solo journey into parenthood, with Darren now the frontrunner in the sperm-donor stakes and Martha anxiously awaiting news of Sam's first attempt at conception.

Rob was the only person Martha felt comfortable talking to about this latest development in Sam's life. In their fifteen-year history of working together, he was a man Martha had learned to trust implicitly. His judgement had proved generally sound— though Martha was sure it was wide of the mark when it came to Constancia. She was perfectly happy to acknowledge that Rob sometimes sensed connections, patterns, nuances that Martha herself might have missed.

Rob was more relaxed than Martha about Sam's aspirations for solo motherhood. 'You'll be joining a growing band of grandparents caught up in far more complicated family arrangements than they had ever anticipated,' he had said during a previous conversation. 'And, by the way, many of them end up playing a very big role in the lives of their grandchildren. Very big and very significant.'

'Somehow that doesn't sound like me,' Martha said.

'Just you wait,' Rob responded. 'I have only one bit of advice: insist on being called Grandma, or some other suitably dignified label. Don't fall for the grandkids calling you Martha. Very trendy, but unwise, I'd say. Harder to maintain the necessary gravitas of the role.'

'Gravitas?' Martha asked. 'Are you sure you're in the right century, Rob?'

This Friday, though, Martha was preoccupied with her misgivings about Sam's use of a Facebook page—*a Facebook page!*—to contact potential donors, and about her apparent determination to handle the actual insemination by herself. Rob heard Martha out, then gently reminded her that her daughter was forty, inviting her to recall how she herself might have felt about parental interference in the decisions she was making when she was forty. 'Samantha's not eighteen, Martha. Not a kid. She's not even twenty-eight.' He generally referred to Martha's daughter as Samantha, though Martha never did, simply because he liked the name.

'Fair point,' Martha said. 'But I sometimes think forty is the new twenty—that's what they used to say about thirty, isn't it? Maybe I'm already the very thing I never wanted to be. Old-fashioned. Out of step with the times.'

'Try to think of this as a good-news story,' Rob said. 'Samantha's young, healthy, bright, talented, and quite well off, from what you tell me. *And* she wants to be a mother. That sounds like pretty cool news for some kid as yet unconceived, wouldn't you say? I can think of a hundred worse scenarios. You know the stats as well as I do.'

'I probably don't, Rob. I used to say that half the women of child-bearing age were desperate to get pregnant, and the other half were desperate not to. It's not as simple as that anymore, is it? People seem to be warier about committing to partners these days. The child question's more complicated than it used to be. It often kicks in too late for Nature's liking. And I hear a lot of "*I* want a child" rather than "*We* want a child". Including from my own daughter, I realise. Is that healthy? Is it good for society in the long run?'

'Society in the long run? God Almighty, Martha, don't take on that burden. We're here to pick up the pieces, remember. Mostly cure, not prevention. No power to reshape the world to our liking.'

'Oh, the world. Has every sixty-seven-year-old in the history of the world thought that things were getting steadily worse? I sometimes remind myself that Socrates thought literacy would spell the end of critical thought. He stubbornly refused to write anything down. Or maybe he couldn't write. I can't remember which. Anyway, long history of us old guys resisting . . . change? Is that all I'm saying?'

Rob shrugged. He was beginning to find Martha's romance with Socrates rather tiresome.

'Old guys?' he repeated. 'How old was Soccers when he carked it?'

'Seventy-one, Rob. Just four years older than I am now. Lordy, it really is time I gave this game away.'

They each took another sip of wine and Rob topped up their glasses.

'But look at the state of the world,' Martha said. 'I mean, the pandemic, for a start. Terrorism, climate change, Ukraine. civil wars, nuclear weapons, drones, America's Space Force—thanks, Donald Trump.'

'Trump! Good God, Martha, let's not go there again. Ever. But if you're going to bleat about politics—'

'Oh, don't get me started. But I'm not imagining it, am I? People's lives do seem to be becoming so much more complicated. More people are in crisis, or think they are. The only reason I've been taking on these new cases, in spite of my theoretical wind-down, is that people have been so desperate to see someone. I know plenty of therapists who are booked out for a year.'

'Good business to be in, eh? Demand outstripping supply?'

'Very droll. But, seriously, is it a good *world* to be in? Pandemics of anxiety and depression—and that's quite apart from the endless mutations of Covid and all the rest. And loneliness. Who do you ever see in here who isn't suffering the effects of some form of social disconnectedness, even if they don't realise it?'

'Steady on, Martha. There are two kinds of people you should never ask about the state of the world—psychotherapists and journalists. Surely you know that! We're the poor buggers who deal with exceptions. We don't get people coming in here purely to let us know how wonderful their relationships are and how their kids are a source of unalloyed pleasure. I don't, anyway. The people I see are the people who *aren't* coping. Why else do they come? They're not psycho-tourists. They need help. That's what gives them the courage to pick up the phone. They're in trouble.'

'Sometimes they're not. Sometimes they're just trying to under-stand themselves a bit better.'

'On the surface, perhaps. And maybe they're the ones who go to analysts, not therapists.'

It was a familiar theme in Rob's reflections on the branch of the profession he was in. For Rob, therapy had to mean solid progress. Martha agreed—wasn't she the great anti-wallowing advocate?—but she was less interested in timelines and boundaries than Rob. She sometimes called him Mister Fixit, not unkindly but not entirely sympathetically. She wasn't sure that, even now, he understood that clients were usually capable of solving their own problems if they were given the time, the space, the encouragement, the support and the affirmation they needed. All Martha wanted for her epitaph was: *She heard us.* Rob wanted more than that.

Rob's point, often repeated, was that if he was doing his job, his clients would soon restabilise and start to get more satisfaction from their lives. And the best sign of that would be when they no longer needed to see him.

'Funny job, isn't it?' he said. 'The measure of our success is the rate at which clients drop *off* our books.'

'Sandrine often says that. She gets quite attached to some of our clients and misses them when they stop coming, though I tell her that it's a good sign. She thinks we should send out little reminders for annual check-ups, like a dentist.'

'Good one, Sandy. But listen, Martha—it's completely ridiculous judging the state of the world by the people who come in here. Or by what you see on news and current affairs shows. *If it bleeds, it leads*: isn't that the journos' catch-cry? Well, if they're wounded or troubled enough—or lost enough—they eventually land on our doorstep.'

'Oh, I suppose you're right, Rob. But I read the journals. So do you.' Martha was still rocked by a study she'd read recently showing that twenty-five per cent of adults reported feeling lonely for most of every week. 'Twenty-five per cent, Rob. You can't ignore a figure like that.'

'True. I'm just asking you to remember that seventy-five per cent of adults *don't* report feeling lonely for most of every week. Sorry to sound like Pollyanna, but you can depress yourself if you don't keep some balance, Martha. When a client leaves here in better shape than when they started, *great*. But we're sending them out to join the majority of people who are rubbing along reasonably contentedly. Occasionally even quite cheerfully. Anyway, living lives at least a notch or two up from miserable.'

'That's a bit grim. Have you been reading Freud again?' It amused Martha that Rob, a committed non-Freudian, would occasionally immerse himself in some of Freud's classics. 'Very clever,' was his recurring verdict. It was meant as faint praise.

'Look, all I'm saying is that when they're through with us, our clients don't join some rarefied, elite group who've been trained up by therapists to function above and beyond. Normal is okay. In fact, that's the definition of okay, isn't it?'

Martha sipped her drink and looked intently at Rob. She couldn't resist the thought that episodes of something close to misery were what Rob himself seemed to be enduring with increasing frequency as his relationship with Constancia staggered towards its inevitable, messy end.

'Uh-oh,' Rob said. 'You've got that Constancia look on your face. Spit it out. What's on your mind?'

'Am I really so transparent? Isn't my face just its usual picture of acceptant tranquillity?' Martha struck an exaggerated pose of yogic meditation.

'Nah, I get it,' Rob said. 'I really do.'

'Get what?'

There was a long silence, and then Rob said: 'Martha, I think I do want to be a father after all.'

That was possibly the last thing Martha had expected to hear.

'A *father*? Where did that come from?'

Another silence.

'It was something Constancia said over lunch a few weeks ago.'

'She wants kids?'

'The opposite. She's just had her tubes tied. No kids. Ever, ever, ever.'

'And?'

'Well, typical Constancia. She said if I wanted to be a father, I'd have to find some other uterus.'

'That's a rather brutally anatomical way of putting it.'

'Constancia all over. Plenty of passion but no romance.'

'And?'

'And what?'

'You really think you might want to be a father after all?'

Paternity again, thought Martha. Sam, Lucas, and now Rob. Was this to be the leitmotif of the final chapter of her working life?

'Never given it much thought before, I guess. Never been the right time. Or the right woman.'

'You have said a few times, over the years, that you'd love a relationship like the one I have with Sam. I remember that.'

'That's true. That *is* true. I would.'

'Sam's hardly been plain sailing, Rob. Never less plain than now. But I know what you mean.'

'Maybe mothers and daughters are different. It wouldn't do to fantasise about what I've been missing. I hear plenty of war stories.'

'Me too.'

'And it's not something you *decide*, really, is it? I mean, did you and Simon ever sit down and say, *Let's have a kid*? Rationally, like that?'

That was a topic almost too painful for Martha to revisit.

'I had a couple of miscarriages before Sam, so there was the assumption . . .'

'Sorry, Martha.'

'It's okay.'

'No, I meant mentioning Simon. Not your favourite subject, I realise.'

Martha turned brisk. 'Look, Rob, there's a lot of truth in what you say. How many first pregnancies are unplanned? Somewhere between a third and a half? Not unwanted, necessarily—just unplanned. In this day and age! So, yeah, you're right. It might not always be a deliberate decision. But what is? All these life choices we're supposed to be making . . . most of them just seem to evolve, don't they?' Martha had often felt that her clients were like bystanders to their own lives, surprised by the way things were turning out.

'Bertrand Russell, here we come.' Rob reached over and picked up a card that sat permanently on his desk. He glanced at it and smiled, then read it aloud: '*Man is a rational animal. So at least we have been told. Throughout a long life I have searched diligently for evidence in favour of this statement. So far, I have not had the good fortune to come across it.*'

'I know. Terrific quote.'

'We should get it framed and hang it in the waiting room.'

'No way. It would seem like an insult. People need to live with the fantasy.'

'That they're rational?'

'Don't you?'

More silence from Rob, yet his clouded face was eloquent.

'Please say what's on your mind, Rob.' Martha was sympathetic. She had wanted three kids and ended up with one. A client she was seeing had only ever wanted one and ended up with three. Two different fathers, the client thinks. How could she not know for sure? Martha wondered.

'At least you tried,' Rob said. 'At least you gave it a go.'

'And you're regretting not having given it a go? This seems a bit sudden, Rob. Mind you, I can easily visualise you as a father. A lovely father, actually.'

'A lovely grandfather, maybe. My brother has just become a grandfather. Well, step-grandfather, anyway, courtesy of his new wife.'

'So, really, it sounds as if Constancia has actually done you a huge favour.'

'Come again?'

'Declaring no babies ever. Go and find another uterus. All that.'

'How is that doing me a favour?'

'Knowing fatherhood is not an option with her forces you to question whether you're ready to live with the idea that the door's been permanently shut. Like being vasectomised.'

Rob looked steadily at Martha.

'Oh, Rob. Let her go.'

SIXTEEN

ON HER THIRD VISIT, RUBY CAME INTO THE RECEPTION area with an uncharacteristically tentative air, as if she was not sure she was welcome, or even expected. Sandrine greeted her warmly and did her best to reassure her that, yes, this was the correct time for her appointment. Martha would be with her in a moment.

Once she was in the room with Martha and settled into her usual chair, she breathed a huge sigh of relief and, unbidden, removed her shoes. Martha sensed that she was more tense and anxious than usual. More troubled, perhaps.

'I see you've taken your shoes off, Ruby. I think that's a good idea. And I have another suggestion. Before we begin our session— or before we start talking, I should say—I'd like to give your feet a short massage. Would that be okay with you? I assure you it will be pleasant, and very relaxing.'

'I guess. Why not?'

'I'll just go and get some oil and a towel—would you mind taking off your stockings while I'm gone?'

Far from feeling more relaxed, Ruby now felt distinctly uneasy. She had really warmed to Martha and felt they'd made some good progress—or, anyway, Ruby felt they'd had some wonderful conversations about all sorts of things she wouldn't normally talk about. But taking off her tights seemed a bit much. Still, she trusted this woman . . .

Martha returned and the massage began. Ruby started to say something and Martha held up her hand to stop her. 'We'll just spend a couple of minutes on this, Ruby, with no talking, okay? Just listen to your breathing and relax all the way from your feet upwards. Listen to what your feet are telling you.'

Martha completed the massage and left Ruby's feet wrapped loosely in the towel.

'You can put your stockings back on before you leave. Now, I wonder where you'd like to start today. Last time, you mentioned that there was one girlfriend in particular who knew more about you than anyone on the planet. I think that's what you said. Would you like to say some more about her?'

'That's Charmaine I'm talking about. I call her Char. She was a school friend, and we lost touch for a few years when we went to different unis, but now we're back to being a bit like we were at school. Lots of laughs. Lots of tears. Close as. What more can I say?'

'Do you feel there are any limits to your conversations with Char? Any boundaries?'

'Never. That's the beautiful thing. Nothing's taboo. She's just split up from her partner, Brian—they never married—and she's unloaded all the details onto me. I've heard the lot. I'm sure he'd freak if he knew half the stuff Char tells me. But she needs to share. *Over*share—that's Char's style.'

'You feel she goes a bit too far sometimes?'

'Oh no, no, no. I never meant that. Oversharing is our kind of sharing. We like to see if it's still possible to shock each other. It isn't. Or not so far. A bit in the beginning, when we first met up again. But not now. We talk about anything—everything. Brian. Vincent. You. Wait till she hears you massaged my feet! Oh, it was lovely. I'm not saying it wasn't. *Really* lovely. But Char will go, *She what?* Fair enough, too. It does sound weird when you just say it. Like, I went in for some counselling and I came out with a foot massage. Is this legit, by the way? Doing my feet as part of *psychology*? Anyway, you're better at it than any of the girls in the nail bar.'

'It's all one, as far as I'm concerned, Ruby. We're not confined to counselling here. I need you to be relaxed with me, so you can talk as freely as you want to. Sometimes we do a bit of deep breathing. Sometimes a little foot massage. Whatever it takes. The main thing is that you're comfortable with it.'

'Oh, yes. *I'm* comfortable. Very. I'm just thinking about Char's reaction.'

'You'll feel it's necessary to tell her?'

'Absolutely. She'll love it. She'll probably get straight on the phone to Sandrine herself to book a foot massage.'

'Well, we don't take bookings for foot massages. But I'm pleased if you think Char will get a charge out of hearing about your experience. When do you see Char? Roughly how often would you speak to each other?'

'We talk every day. Some days two or three times. Depends what's happening. We have lunch once a week—Wednesdays, while Vincent is off with his *therapist*. Maybe a coffee on the spur of the moment. Maybe a drink after work on Fridays if there's nothing doing in my office. She thinks I should bed Jerry. You know Jerry, my friend at work? No way I'd ever even think about that. Not with Jerry. Don't fuck your friends. Wasn't that Timi Haze?'

'I think Gore Vidal might have said it first.'

'Who? Anyway, that's the sort of game Char likes to play. Halfway between teasing and shocking. Know what I mean?'

'But she's not serious, you mean?'

'You'd never know with Char. What a case!'

'So perhaps she knows more about your relationship with Vincent than I do?'

'Way more. *Way* more.'

'And do you think Vincent has any idea of the closeness between you and Char?'

'Where are you going with this, Martha? Are you being tricky all of a sudden?'

'Tricky? Not in the slightest, Ruby. It's a pretty obvious thing for me to raise. Let me spell it out even more clearly. Do you think Vincent might feel about Char the way you feel about his therapist? The intimacy. The frankness. The secrecy. That kind of thing.'

Ruby fell silent. She looked at Martha, then looked away. She reached down and wrapped the towel more tightly around her feet.

Then she said: 'That's a bit *too* obvious, isn't it? A bit too neat? Like, I'm all for the simplest explanation—that's a big part of my job. Finding the most simple and elegant solutions. If it's too complicated in theory, it won't work in practice. But Char's my friend. I wouldn't mind if Vincent had a mate as close as Char is to me. That would be good. That would be healthy. But *paying a therapist* to talk about your wife? Come on, there's no comparison.'

'I thought we were trying to operate as if we believe Vincent when he says that his therapy isn't all about you?'

Ruby fell silent again. Then she unwrapped the towel, stood up and announced that she'd go to the washroom and put her tights back on. 'I need to pee, anyway,' she said.

Martha swivelled her chair around to face her desk and made some notes on Ruby's file. Then she stood up and walked to the window. It was a cold, clear day, with just a hint of blossom starting to appear on the only two trees that remained from the original garden of the cottage. Spring would bring its usual raft of new cases, Martha reflected. Pandemic or no pandemic, winter exaggerated people's gloom. Spouses could start to seem duller than usual. Were people who travelled north for winter breaks trying to warm up their relationship? Checking herself, Martha wondered if she might be becoming jaded herself, being tempted by such a glib, simplistic interpretation. Definitely time to think about pulling the plug . . .

Ruby was back in the room, looking fresh and feisty.

'You still seem to be missing the main point, Martha,' she said.

'Which is?'

'If it's not about me, he'd be comfortable telling me what it *is* about. Isn't that true?'

'Look, Ruby, I won't push the Char analogy too far, but it sounds as if there are a million things you talk to Char about—things that have nothing to do with Vincent—that you nevertheless wouldn't pass on to Vincent. Am I right? *Strictly girl talk?* I think you used those very words at our first session together.'

'Yeah, okay, but you said it yourself—those are things that have nothing to do with Vincent.'

'But other things *are* about him?'

'Yeah. Some.'

'And that might include some things you don't discuss with him, either?'

'Stop right there, Martha. Have you even been listening? I've tried and tried and *tried* to talk about all kinds of stuff with Vincent but he just clams up. Not interested. Then he pays someone—he *pays* someone—to talk about all the stuff I'd love him to talk about with me.'

Martha nodded and smiled at Ruby. 'Our time's up for today, I'm afraid, but I'd like you to think about this for next week: on your very first visit, you said you were coming to see me as a form of self-defence, to find out what really went on between a client and a counsellor—or therapist—that Vincent seemed unable to share with you. So can you imagine the possibility— I'm not saying it *is* possible, I'm just asking you to imagine—that Vincent might have started seeing his therapist as a defence against the intimacy he suspects you have with Char? Maybe *he's* been feeling a bit left out?'

'Totally different thing. Friends. Therapists. Totally different.'

'But that might be the point, Ruby. They might indeed be totally different. And so might spouses and therapists.'

'I'm not sure you really get it, Martha. But, yeah, I'll think about that.'

SEVENTEEN

TWO OR THREE TIMES A YEAR, MARTHA INVITED A HANDFUL of clients to join her for afternoon tea in what had once been the dining room of the cottage. She liked the idea of giving a few carefully chosen clients an opportunity to relate to each other—and to her—in a purely social setting. She had also found, over the years, that helpful connections were sometimes made at these little events between people who had been feeling socially isolated. It was an idea she had originally borrowed from a GP friend who started turning on Christmas lunch for patients who lived alone and had nowhere else to go at Christmas.

The afternoon teas were usually held on a Saturday, just for an hour or so. Martha's only stipulation was that there should be no discussion of clinical issues, and no reference to anything covered in the clients' sessions with Martha. When she issued these invitations, Martha stressed that there was absolutely no hidden agenda. It wasn't a trick. It wasn't a 'strategy'. It was just what it appeared to be—Martha Elliott inviting a few of her new clients to meet informally over a cup of tea or coffee, and maybe get to know each other a little. In Martha's mind, her afternoon teas were a simple gift to her clients, and they were free to respond however they liked.

Rob didn't approve of this idea. In fact, he strongly disapproved of it. He thought it inherently risky to introduce an element of such personal familiarity to the relationship between therapist and client. Yet Martha's experience had taught her that these modest, one-off social encounters gave her a quite different—and potentially valuable—insight into the lives of people she otherwise saw only as clients.

In spite of his disapproval, Rob had agreed, as he usually did— but always at the last minute, as a symbolic protest—to assist in setting up the space and arranging the furniture. Sandrine usually helped out with the preparation of food on these occasions, but she was occupied with grandchildren this time, so Martha had gratefully accepted Sam's offer to step in. She welcomed this opportunity to spend an hour with her daughter.

After pondering the list of possible guests, Martha had eventually decided to invite only her three newest clients—Lucas, Ruby and Hazel. Partners? Well, that would be up to them. She always made the offer, but her clients usually elected to come on their own.

She had found it hard to imagine the Ortons accepting an invitation like this, though she rather liked the idea of seeing how they related to each other in a social setting. At the eleventh hour, she decided to invite them too.

Ruby accepted with alacrity, but said Vincent would be 'an apology'. Martha wondered whether Ruby had even invited him. Hazel was similarly keen, once Martha had assured her, several times, that there would be no discussion at all of any subjects raised in their private sessions.

Lucas was grateful for the invitation and, for a few days, was equivocal about whether Rani and Felix would join him. In the end, he said he would like to bring Felix, if the others would be okay with having a three-year-old in their midst.

A message from Bill Orton said that he would come but that Abigail was 'otherwise occupied', which sounded to Martha rather as if she might be watching television.

An hour before the guests were due, Sam arrived with a plate of pastries and tarts from Oscar's, a new patisserie just across Victoria Avenue. Under strict instructions from Martha, she began making sandwiches. Once Rob arrived, a little later than promised, he moved the table and chairs into position and helped Sam set the table and lay out the food. With much laughter, they addressed each other as 'Ms Elliott' and 'Dr Nielsen', and loudly criticised each other's placement of items on the table. When Rob started making origami shapes out of the paper napkins, instead of folding them as Martha had requested, her initial amusement at their banter turned to irritation. She was also mildly resentful of the fact that she was getting almost no personal time with Sam herself.

Martha had decided that Sam and Rob should disappear before the first of the guests arrived and so, at a quarter to three, when everything was prepared to her satisfaction, she sent them off together for a late lunch at Oscar's, her shout.

The first to arrive was Hazel, a few minutes before three o'clock, bearing a small plate of scones, though Martha had told people not to bring anything. Then Ruby arrived, with a bottle of chilled white wine—'Just in case,' she said. Hazel and Ruby began chatting while Martha went into the kitchen to put the wine in the fridge and make tea for Hazel, coffee for Ruby. She was reassured by the sound of laughter from both women, and when she returned to the table she found Hazel regaling Ruby with tales from her years as a kindergarten teacher.

'The children were delightful, of course; it was the parents who were the real problem,' Hazel was saying. 'Though I'm told it's far worse today than it ever used to be. Regular email reports on every child. Videos of classroom activities. Madness. Oh, and half the children have to be fed when they arrive because they haven't had breakfast.'

'That can't be everywhere, surely,' Ruby said. 'Although I do remember some kids in my primary school whose families couldn't afford new shoes for them.'

'Oh, I don't think this is a case of money. I think it's time, dear. They're all so *busy* these days. Like my son—he's in *Hollywood*, would you believe.'

Ruby seemed sufficiently impressed by that piece of information to satisfy Hazel.

'Do you have any little ones yourself, Ruby?' Hazel asked.

'Not yet, I'm afraid. I'd like one, at least, but, well, we're not yet properly set up for it, really. My husband says we need to be better established before we start a family. I don't know, though.'

'Don't wait, Ruby, would be my advice. The female body is built to bear children at a young age, dear. All these girls waiting till they're in their thirties. Harder to conceive. More complicated pregnancies. Less energy for running around after littlies.'

Martha was surprised by the strength of Hazel's convictions on the subject and by her uninhibited relaying of them to Ruby who, Martha knew, was already into her mid-thirties. She could have been mildly offended, but seemed not to be. She looked as if she found Hazel's concern rather touching.

And then Lucas arrived, holding the hand of the three-year-old Felix. They stood together at the edge of the room and, even when Martha urged them to come and sit down—she'd borrowed a highchair for Felix—they hesitated. It was hard to tell who was the more reluctant. They were both dressed in denim jeans, with matching red jumpers over their white shirts. Considering the dramatic difference in their height, the matching clothes produced a slightly comical effect. Hazel gave a little clap of delight.

'Come on in, Lucas,' Martha said. 'Hello, Felix.'

Felix looked at the three women, then at Lucas, then back at the women, and his bottom lip trembled. Hazel was instantly out of her chair, greeting Felix warmly, scooping him into her arms and carrying him, pressed to her chest, back to her seat. She settled him on her knee and began quietly, privately, talking to him, playing a game with his fingers and then softly singing him a nursery rhyme, as if they were the only two people in the entire world. Felix was mesmerised.

Lucas explained to Martha that Rani had decided to use the time alone to do some household chores and have a rest. Then he took a seat next to Ruby and, bypassing pleasantries, asked her what work she did. They quickly established that they had both been in the engineering faculty at Sydney University, Ruby just a few years ahead of Lucas. Martha, pleased by all this rapid engagement, went to fetch a glass of milk for Felix and a mug of coffee for Lucas.

There was still no sign of Bill Orton.

⁓

After half an hour, serious inroads had been made into the food, and the mood had mellowed. Lucas offered Felix the highchair, but he shook his head vigorously and, laughing, burrowed his face into Hazel's chest.

'He's a very good talker, Lucas,' Hazel remarked across the table. No one else had been paying much attention to what Felix might have been saying—he had eyes only for Hazel, and an appetite only for her scones. 'He knows "Incy Wincy Spider", don't you, Felix? Let's sing it together.'

And so they did. Ruby had tears in her eyes. Lucas was beaming with obvious pride.

After a few minutes more, Hazel announced that Felix had had enough sitting around chatting and needed to go outside and play.

'Why don't we walk up to Beauchamp Park?' she suggested. 'I have a very bouncy rubber ball in my bag. Never go anywhere without a ball in my bag. If you have a ball to bounce, you're never bored. Who wants to come?'

'Let's all go,' Martha said. 'I can clean this up later. Lucas, there's only one sandwich left on the plate—surely you can save its life?'

Lucas obliged. Ruby grabbed another lemon tart.

'Toilet?' Hazel asked Felix, who ignored the question and headed for the door. Nothing was going to distract him from a park and a ball *and* a new playmate who seemed to know all the songs he knew.

They set off in the direction of the park, Hazel and Ruby each holding one of Felix's hands, occasionally swinging him back and forth as they walked, with frequent shouts of 'More!' from Felix. Martha and Lucas walked together behind the others.

'Kind of like the ultimate offsite,' Lucas said with a grin.

⁓

It was almost five o'clock when they returned to the cottage to find Bill Orton standing outside, clutching a bottle of wine and consulting his watch.

'Hello, Bill,' Martha said as she unlocked the door and let the others in.

'Have I missed something?' he asked.

'Oh, we just took little Felix up to the park for a bit of play. It was fun. That's all you missed. And the food. We ate before we went there.'

Bill frowned. 'Abby told me drinks at five,' he said.

'Really? No, no, it was afternoon tea at three. But come in and meet the others.' She took the bottle from Bill. 'Looks as if it could be drinks at five, after all.'

EIGHTEEN

SAMANTHA AND ROB'S CONVERSATION OVER LUNCH AT Oscar's patisserie had begun as a warm, animated but uncontroversial continuation of the rather flippant, playful manner they'd adopted earlier in the afternoon. That had made it easy for them to connect, given that this was to be the first sustained conversation they'd ever had. They had known each other in passing for such a long time that they might perhaps have called themselves friends rather than mere acquaintances, but they were certainly not intimates.

They had finished eating and drained their coffee cups when their attention was caught by the sound of a hungry cry from a baby at a nearby table. As they watched the parents fussing over their tot, Samantha and Rob both seemed lost in the moment. And then, as if controlled by the same impulse, they turned back and looked at each other rather self-consciously.

There was an awkward silence, broken by Samantha: 'Have you thought about having—'

'Yes,' Rob said, unintentionally cutting her off. 'Well, yes and no. I mean, not officially. It's been difficult . . .'

'I know exactly what you mean.' Samantha sighed and gave a little shrug. 'Actually—and this is a little embarrassing; I'm not sure I should even be telling you—I've been ready for the big leap into motherhood for a while now, and I'm currently . . . well, I'm actually looking for a donor. Finding one is a lot more difficult than you might think!'

She laughed nervously and Rob responded with a chuckle and a sympathetic nod. 'Go on,' he said. 'No need to be embarrassed.'

Rob had heard snatches of the story from Martha but now, hearing Samantha's gloomy litany of failed attempts, he heard himself say—recklessly, lightly, almost as a throwaway line: 'Maybe I could be your donor.'

The words hung in the air between them, and they both froze with evident embarrassment. Then they laughed, and the moment passed. After an awkward pause, they stood to leave. As they parted, there was a tentative hug that had felt to both of them like a way of saying: *To be continued?*

Samantha had known Rob ever since he'd joined her mother in the practice fifteen years earlier. She had been in her mid-twenties back then. There had been no hint of a romantic spark: they had both been in relationships at the time and, in any case, Rob had seemed to Samantha like an 'older man'. But she had always liked him, and she knew how highly Martha valued him as a colleague. Their occasional, incidental encounters had been comfortable and undemanding. She was intrigued by the fact that he, alone among her friends and acquaintances, invariably called her 'Samantha'. She secretly enjoyed that; it felt like a sign of his respect for her, but also a kind of joke—the way she sometimes called Martha 'Mother' with mock formality.

But romance? It had never crossed her mind. Or his.

Until that lunch.

Neither of them had let go of Rob's *maybe*. Samantha had resolved that she would find a pretext for them to meet again, privately, perhaps over another lunch, just to check whether she had misread the moment. She was already starting to see Rob in a very different light, as a very different person from the one she'd known all those years. Quite apart from that *maybe*, their conversation at Oscar's had morphed so easily from banter to intimacy, she wanted to be certain he wasn't playing the professional counsellor, responding to her all-too-apparent neediness. She hated it when her mother slipped into clinical mode. The tone of voice. The head bent slightly forward. The earnest receptivity. She knew the signs. Surely Rob hadn't been playing that game. But she had to know. Already, there seemed the potential for magic.

Rob, too, had experienced the *maybe* moment as significant. He had scarcely dared hope that the giddying tilt he felt at that point in the conversation with Samantha was as real, as destabilising, for her as it was for him. But he had known he would have to test it and see where it might lead. It was as if Samantha had suddenly, surprisingly, emerged from the shadows of simply being 'Martha's daughter' and now appeared to him as a symbol of something fresh and new and lovely. Perhaps—he later thought—he was sensing the enchanting prospect of a radically different life.

He had also known, in that moment, that he must be free of Constancia—finally and forever. That entire journey now seemed unendurably torrid and ultimately pointless. Why had he put up with it so far beyond its blindingly apparent use-by date? He no longer had any need to answer that question. His focus had shifted. Whether or not the sudden dream of a life with Samantha would ever become a reality, Constancia now appeared to him as a parody of herself. The femme fatale had become *une femme pathétique.*

NINETEEN

ABIGAIL WAS SITTING ON THE BACK VERANDAH SCROLLING through her messages when Bill returned home from Martha's gathering.

'Well, you stuffed that up big-time,' he said.

'What are you on about, Bill?'

'Drinks at five, you told me. It was actually afternoon tea at three. Spot the deliberate mistake.'

'You malign me, dear heart. I wasn't paying that much attention. Drinks at five, afternoon tea at three—what's the difference? Who has afternoon tea at three, anyway?'

'Well, your little plot backfired. Another one of the group had also brought wine, and they came back at five and we all had rather a jolly time.'

'Came back? Back from what?'

'Some local park. There was a little boy involved. Indian-looking kid. Nice little fella. Felix. They all took him to this park to run around a bit. Throw a ball. I dunno.'

'Oh, what a pity you missed that! Sounds like heaven—running around *and* throwing a ball. You could have had a coronary on the spot. I did you a favour, by the sound of it.'

Bill went inside, changed into old clothes, then returned and said to Abigail: 'I'm going to mount an assault on the shed. A lot of stuff needs clearing out. I don't want anything to eat, thanks.'

'I wasn't offering anything. I ate long before you got home. What were you doing all that time, anyway? Two hours of drinkies with a collection of nutters?'

'This may come as a surprise to you, Abby, but I actually met some rather pleasant young people.'

'Young? How young?'

'Thirties, I'd say. One was the very pale-skinned father of the Indian boy, so there's a backstory there. The other one, a woman, was an engineer. Fully liberated, as you might expect.'

'God, how did she cope with *you*?'

'I'll ignore that. There was also an older woman there. Very tight with the kid. I couldn't quite make out the connection. Anyway, good people all. Not a nutter in sight.'

'And Martha Elliott?'

'Playing the hostess to a tee. Very warm, very welcoming—even to a bloke who turned up two hours late, courtesy of his wife's Freudian whatsit.'

'How cosy you make it all sound.'

Bill fell silent, wondering whether there was any point in going on. Eventually, he sat down beside Abigail and turned to look at her.

'Abby, I felt like a total fraud at that drinks party. As if I was there under false pretences. I mean, they were all clients, and we're *not* clients. Not in any real sense. Two visits—well, only one, really. That first visit was just some kind of pantomime. And even the second visit was a farce.'

'What are you trying to say, Bill? Spit it out.'

'This may surprise you, but I have developed some respect for Martha. I like her. She's a good person. I saw that this afternoon. All that stuff you went on with the first time we met her, practically accusing her of hypocrisy—where did that come from? She strikes me as the most *un*hypocritical person I've ever met.'

'I didn't accuse her of anything. Not yet, anyway. I just made some general observations.'

'Go easy is all I'm saying. If you push her too hard, she'll just refuse to see us, and then where would your little scheme be? In tatters.'

'Oh, she won't get a chance to do that, Bill. Our next visit will be our last. I promised you that. But we do need to see this through to the bitter end, and so does she. Justice will be done. You watch.'

'Maybe I should just pull out and leave you to carry on with this by yourself. You two, I should say—I imagine it's the Dark Twin who's calling the shots. Why should I be involved?'

'But I *need* you, Bill. We signed up for couples therapy, remember, and you need an actual couple to make that look convincing.'

'There you go again. *To make that look convincing.* I really don't want to go on with this. I turned up once and found myself humiliated. I turned up again and listened to you being embarrassingly offensive. That's enough. I've got half a mind to go and see Martha Elliott on my own. Fess up. Tell her how uncomfortable I felt about being there and how deceptive we're being.'

'That's your problem right there, Bill: you've got half a mind. You've lost the other half.' Abigail stood and glared at her husband. 'If you go and see her on your own, I'll be very, very angry. You promised me your full support. *Promised* me. Remember? Don't you *dare* go to see Martha Elliott on your own. Okay? Do I have your word?'

Bill shrugged. 'I guess,' he said, shaking his head in bewilderment, as puzzled by his own acquiescence as by Abigail's real intentions.

'In any case,' Abigail said, 'you shouldn't feel too bad. I imagine half the people who see Martha Elliott are not telling the truth, even when they might be trying to. And what about those who actually set out to deceive her? Deliberately misrepresenting their situation—to get her sympathy, maybe. Or her support, for whatever reason. Recruit her to their team.'

Bill snorted with derision. 'That's bullshit, Abby, and you know it. I'm certain Martha would expect her clients to *try* to tell her the truth. If people are just pretending, what's the point? Are you saying the whole thing is a wank?'

'All the world's a stage, Bill. *And all the men and women merely players.* Get with the program. Everyone's putting on a show, one way or another. Trying to make themselves look better than they are. Or different, anyway. Worse, sometimes, if they're determined to play the victim. But mostly better. Ever heard of spin? Politics runs on it. And why do you think there's a cosmetics industry?'

'You're mad, Abby. Mad.'

'See? That's a lie. I'm actually dangerously sane. But it makes *you* feel better to say I'm mad. Lying often has that effect.'

Bill started to speak, then gave up.

After a moment's silence, Abigail said: 'Go and clean out the shed, Bill.'

'I've changed my mind. I'm going to watch a movie.'

'Then put some clean clothes on, please. I'm not having you sit on the couch in those filthy things.'

Bill looked at his wife with barely concealed contempt. *Was she really worth it?* he wondered for the hundredth time.

'I've changed my mind again. I'll be in the shed if you need me.'

⁓

Sitting on the verandah, Abigail thought that, if nothing else, this whole episode had reinforced her growing conviction that Bill was never going to become the man she had wanted him to be. Not courageous enough. Not edgy enough. Not imaginative enough. And, when it counted, not tough enough. Not enough *fight* in him. She would insist he accompanied her to the final session with Martha Elliott and after that . . . well, maybe it would be time for a radical rethink. Life would be simpler and less stressful without him. For a start, she wouldn't have to defend herself at every turn. She knew she was on the high moral ground in her looming showdown with Martha Elliott, but she wasn't confident Bill would ever see it that way: he seemed to her to be stranded in the moral foothills.

⁓

Cleaning out the shed, Bill recalled that Abigail had said her scheme to bring Martha Elliott undone could be fun and might even be productive for them. Well, it wasn't fun, but there had already been one productive outcome for Bill. He now knew, with a certainty he'd previously managed to evade, that his life with Abigail was unsustainable. He had thought her other qualities made her arrogance bearable, but he had been wrong. She was as irredeemably self-righteous as her sister. Trying to make this marriage work had been like trying to fill a bath with the plug pulled out.

⁓

Hi Gabs
Just about at the end of my tether with Bill. Too nosy.
Too antsy. I need him to see us thru to the end of
Operation Elliott. After that? Kaput, methinks.
Abs xox

> *Know what u mean, Abs. Himself has his problems,*
> *but life ain't dull. Call me.*
> *Gabs xox*

TWENTY

RUBY'S NEXT APPOINTMENT FELL IN THE WEEK FOLLOWING the afternoon tea. Martha generally found these post-social sessions helpful—there was often an easier, more relaxed tone, and useful talking points sometimes emerged from the conversations with other clients. In Ruby's case, a broad smile announced a distinct lightening of her spirits.

'I wore pants and knee-highs today, so there'd be no drama about getting my tights off.'

'Breathing first, then feet,' Martha said, returning the smile, and they did a short deep-breathing routine together.

As Martha worked on her feet, Ruby reported that her friend Char had, as predicted, hooted at the news that Martha was combining counselling with a foot massage. 'She wants to know if it's strictly legal,' Ruby said with a laugh.

'Legal? What a strange question. Nothing illegal about it. Maybe a trifle irregular. But, sure, legal. As long as the client gives her consent. And I am a qualified reflexologist, Ruby, as well as a psychologist.' Martha pointed to both certificates on her office wall.

'That's what I told Char. Anyway, the switch from skirt and tights to pants and knee-highs is a pretty clear sign of consent, isn't it?'

They lapsed into an easy silence while Martha finished the massage and wrapped Ruby's feet in a towel.

'So, tell me what's been on your mind.'

Ruby's face clouded briefly, then brightened.

'Bit of good news to start. You'll never guess what Vincent and I did on Sunday.'

'I won't even try.'

'We went to a toy store and bought a bouncy ball, just like Hazel's. Then I took Vincent to Beauchamp Park. A kind of rerun. You know what? It totally relaxed him. We chucked the ball back and forth a bit. Then he tried kicking it, which was a riot—it went everywhere but where he meant it to go. Mostly it was throwing and catching. Amazing how out of practice we were. And how hot and sweaty you get, just throwing a ball. Neither of us has ever been what you'd call sporty, but it was high-voltage fun. So, thanks to Hazel. And thanks to you. Oh, and also, I tried making scones when we got back from the park. Total flop. They turned out like rock cakes. I need Hazel's recipe.'

Ruby sat back in her chair.

'Also, I had a really, really good chat to Lucas at your afternoon tea. We both did engineering at Sydney. Did you know that? What a coincidence! But he's having a tough time at home. You probably do know all about that. Oh, I hope you didn't mind me bringing wine. I thought it might help loosen things up a bit. It certainly loosened Lucas up.'

Martha remained impassive. She wondered just how much Lucas had told Ruby. She hoped he hadn't strayed too far into his problems with Rani. This was not what she expected or intended to happen at the afternoon tea, but neither was the wine. Perhaps Lucas was only capable of talking about what was on his mind. He was certainly no master of small talk.

'I didn't say much about Vincent, though. What is there to say? I did mention to that lovely Bill Orton that my husband was also seeing a counsellor, and it was a bit of a thing between us.'

'Is that something you'd normally discuss with people, Ruby?'

'Oh, no. No way. Except Char, of course. No, I just mentioned it to Bill because he seemed such a decent chap. Sort of a father-figure type. And it was, like, a natural thing to mention. We were only there because we were all seeing you. Bill said the counselling was a bit of a thing between him and his wife as well. We didn't pursue it, though. Nothing indiscreet. All good. You're looking worried, Martha.'

'Not worried, exactly. But . . . well . . . I just hope you didn't feel as if you said too much. More than you wanted to. Or more than you might have said without the wine.' Martha tried to soften her remark with a smile.

'God, no. I can hold my grog. Engineering, remember?'

'Anyway, let's get back to Vincent, shall we? You were going to give some thought to the possibility that he might have started seeing a therapist as a defence against your intimacy with Char. Just as an idea to play with. Do you remember?'

'I do remember. And don't you see the logical contradiction in that idea? Or the circularity, maybe. Sorry to sound blunt. Jerry says I can sound blunt. But if Vincent was seeing someone because he felt shut out of my relationship with Char—which would be fair enough—then that would mean the sessions with his fancy therapist *were* about me.'

'I notice you said that would be fair enough. You've shifted a bit, Ruby?'

'Yeah, a bit. Seeing Vince running after that ball. Hearing him cursing himself like a kid when he missed a catch or sent a kick flying off into the trees. I mean, the guy's *human*, right? He's a kind of lovable bear. And I thought, watching him rushing about like a mad thing, there's so much about me this guy doesn't know. Stuff I talk to Char about. Stuff I talk to you about. Even some of the stuff I said to Lucas. You can't know everything about another person. Not even your nearest and dearest. I get that.'

'And do you get that it might be important for Vincent to have someone he can confide in, even if it *is* sometimes about you? Maybe things you've said or done, or not done, that he wants to process without necessarily wanting to confront you about them?'

'Yeah, I do get that. I really do. At least, I think I do. But I'll never forgive him for covering it up. Or for being so damned secretive about it.'

'And if Vincent asked you what you'd talked to Char about one day when you'd had a drink with her after work, what would you say?'

'I'd say, *Mind your own business*. I *have* said it. With a laugh, though. Not like, *Mind your own fucking business*. Just light. He gets the idea of girl talk. I think he only ever asks because he'd love to know what girl talk really means. I think he imagines we talk about gynaecology all the time. As if.'

Ruby smiled at her own remark.

'To tell you the truth, Martha, I think he knows we talk about the men in our life. Or our mothers. Our difficult sisters. And, yeah, even a bit of gynaecology. Or obstetrics, anyway. We both want kids. Now Char has ditched Brian, she's starting all over again. What a gruesome prospect.'

'Ruby, it sounds as if you saw Vincent in a different light when you were playing in the park with him. Did you want to say anything else about that?'

'Not really. It's kind of private. I mean, I think he saw *me* in a different light. Vince can be really lovely, you know. He was certainly more . . . more amorous. Even though I was so sweaty.'

'By all means keep the private part of the story to yourself. That goes without saying. Just one other thing. Do you think you'd feel better about Vincent sharing stuff with a friend rather than with his therapist?'

Ruby considered this. 'That's a curly one. I think . . . well, I don't know. I think it would all depend what sort of stuff it was. I don't think I would have a problem with him talking to a mate the way I talk to Char. But I can see that, yes, there might be some things where he feels he needs professional advice he couldn't get from a mate over a beer. Obviously.'

'Go on, Ruby.'

Ruby's face had fallen. The buoyancy had left her.

'We're right back where we started, Martha. Do we really need to go there again? I get that Vincent needs to talk to someone who isn't me. Isn't just a mate. I really do. And it's better between us when I don't say a single word about it. I didn't mention it on Sunday. Not once. I'm sure that was a relief for him. I was quite proud of myself. But I ask myself over and over: if it's not about me, and he can't talk to me about it, what *is* it about? Is there something serious going on? Is he in some kind of trouble? What's so *secret*?'

'There's a difference between private and secret, Ruby. He might need a little time each week for some private reflections or ruminations, and he might find his therapist a helpful companion for that process. Maybe he's not good at doing that kind of work on his own. A lot of people need help with it. It doesn't mean it's *secret* work, Ruby—just private. Does that make any sense to you?'

'There's stuff going on he doesn't want to share with me? Is that what you're saying?'

'I'm saying more than that, Ruby. I'm saying that some people— actually, I think it applies to all of us—can benefit from some regular personal reflection on our life. Our relationships. Our dreams. The sources of sadness or disappointment. How we're doing in general. Some people do it brilliantly on their own. Some people do it with a close friend, maybe the way you do with Char. Some people use a therapist who's trained for precisely that kind of work. Maybe that's Vincent's situation. We can't be everything to each other, in a friendship or even in a marriage. If Vincent started expecting you to be his therapist, that would change the dynamics of your marriage quite a lot, wouldn't it? If you expected him to be just like Char is, what would be special about your relationship with her?'

'Special. Yeah. Good point. And Vince . . .'

'Go on, Ruby.'

'He *is* special, Martha.'

Martha sensed there was nothing more to be said, for now, and she let the silence expand to fill the few remaining minutes of the session.

As Ruby put her shoes back on, she said: 'You won't forget to ask Hazel for that scone recipe, will you? See you next week.'

TWENTY-ONE

'AND WHAT, EXACTLY, MIGHT YOU BE UP TO?'

Constancia had come home earlier than Rob had been expecting. She found him leaning over an overnight bag on the bed, filling it with clothes and a few books he had left at her place.

Rob said nothing.

'Robin! Speak to me. Are you going away? Are *we* going away? *Ooh*, how exciting! Where are we off to? Will I need a summer or winter wardrobe? Wait a minute—don't tell me you need more *space*. Not again, surely.'

Rob straightened his back and turned to face Constancia. Out of his trouser pocket he withdrew a pair of gaudily patterned underpants, unmistakably male, and held them out to Constancia.

'Oh, that's Terry. Don't tell me he didn't put his underpants back on. He did leave in rather a hurry. Still, that's a bit disgusting.'

'Terry?'

'You know about Terry. I've told you about our meaningless liaisons. I know you don't approve, but you've never really objected. Actually, I even wondered if you rather liked the idea. I mean, you're the psychologist: aren't some men turned on by the thought of their woman going at it with another bloke? Maybe you'd like to watch some time?'

'Turned on? Constancia, let me tell you something. I couldn't give a damn about Terry . . . or Jerry or Kerry or Harry or Barry. I'm done here. Visiting rights relinquished. Not interested. I half thought you were making up those little tales of Constancia the Conquistadora, but I see they were real. Or maybe some of them were. Tell someone who cares.'

'Oh, Robin, surely you're not throwing a tantrum over Terry's tacky undies?'

'No, Constancia. It's not a tantrum. And I only came across them when I was reaching under the bed for any stray socks of mine. I'm leaving, Constancia. Just as you requested . . . as recently as last night, in case you've forgotten.'

'Last night? That must have been the Fernet *con* Coca talking. Too much Fernet and not enough Coca. My head *was* a bit sore this morning . . .'

'Constancia, listen. I'm leaving. *Vamoose*, you said. You're looking at a man in the very act of vamoosing.'

'Oh, Robbie, you can't be serious. You have such a sad little face.' Constancia took a step towards Rob.

He flinched and turned away from her.

'Do you remember saying you could sense the end was nigh? Constancia? Do you remember saying that? Several times? *Many* times? Well, you were right. It was nigh. And now it's arrived. In fact, if we're honest, it arrived some time ago.'

Constancia stood with her hands on her hips. 'Ha. Take a break, by all means. More *space*. You'll be back, just like all those other times.' Her tone had darkened into mockery. 'Oh, yes, you go and crawl into a hole somewhere and lick those terrible wounds I apparently inflicted on you last night. Then, when you're all better, you'll be back. And you know why? Because you can't live without me. You're pathetic, really. I don't know why I bother.'

Rob closed his bag and carried it to the front door of the apartment. Constancia had retreated to the bathroom. Then he remembered a jacket that was still hanging in the wardrobe and went back to fetch it. Still no sign of Constancia. He hesitated on the threshold and then, as he headed for the lift, he heard the door click shut behind him. They had not said goodbye. He had not returned her key.

He went back to the apartment door and knocked.

'Back already?' Constancia exclaimed, standing inside the half-opened door in her black—always black—underwear, mobile pressed to her ear. 'Perfect timing,' she said. 'Look at me. I was just getting ready for my bath.'

'I need to give you this,' Rob said, handing her the key.

She flung it back at him and slammed the door.

He left the key where it lay in the corridor. Carried his bag into the lift. Descended to the garage. Threw the bag onto the back seat of his car and drove away.

TWENTY-TWO

AS SOON AS LUCAS WALKED THROUGH THE DOOR, MARTHA sensed trouble. His cheery disposition at the afternoon tea, three weeks ago now, had deserted him. This was the first time Martha had seen him since then—he had cancelled two appointments and made this one at short notice.

He removed his shoes and jacket and loosened his tie. A brief, almost fake smile in Martha's direction.

'Hello, Lucas,' she said. 'It's been a while. Good to see you again. Shall we begin with a few breathing exercises?'

'If you insist,' Lucas said, sounding sullen.

'Well, no, Lucas, I don't *insist*. It's entirely up to you. But I do find it can be a good way to begin, especially if someone arrives here feeling a little tense.'

'A *little* tense? Ha.'

'Come on, then, let's do some breathing together. Okay?'

More out of politeness than any real conviction, Lucas acquiesced. Martha encouraged him to close his eyes, and she continued the exercises for longer than she usually did, gradually tapering off the deep breathing and lowering her voice to a murmur.

Lucas seemed to relax, and Martha remained silent until he was ready to open his eyes and engage with her.

'Tell me what's on your mind, Lucas,' she said quietly.

'My metaphorical mind! I hardly know where to start. Aren't people complicated? I mean, in my work, I can usually find really neat solutions to knotty problems. I was chatting to Ruby about it at your offsite.' He smiled as he repeated that little joke. 'I suppose it was actually an *on*site, wasn't it? Except for the park. Anyway. The good news about *that* is that Hazel is taking the boy two days a week—Tuesdays and Thursdays. They are in love with each other. I drop him off before work and pick him up on my way home. I was sure it would be too much for her, but she says not. She's trying to persuade me to make it three days a week. She offered when we were at the park, after she discovered that Rani and I both have full-time jobs and the little fella spends every weekday at childcare. So, this is only the third week of the arrangement. I offered to pay her for her time, but she wouldn't hear of it. She actually seemed slightly offended. Anyway, it's taken a bit of re-strategising, but I think it's going to be permanent. Ha. What am I saying? Is *anything* permanent?'

Martha had never seen Lucas in such a state before. Almost wild-eyed. He was clearly happy about the advent of Hazel in Felix's life, but there was a sharp edge even to the way he was describing this welcome development.

'They read lots of stories and sing all his favourite songs. And he has a rest in the morning and a nap in the afternoon. He's become a real chatterbox. He calls her Hazy, which is precisely the opposite of what she is, wouldn't you say? Sharp as. If she was fifty years younger, I'd marry her.'

'Except that you're already married,' Martha said with a smile.

'Yes, there is that. I guess.'

'You guess?'

'Well, how can I put this?' A long pause. No eye contact. 'Felix Kumar is back in town.'

'Oh.'

'Yes. Oh. Indeed, *oh*.'

'Permanently? Another secondment?'

'Oh, nothing as serious as that. Just a one-week visit. He's gone now. I said he *is* back in town. I meant *was*. Feels like *is*, though.'

'Rani saw him?'

'Multiple times.'

'And?'

'And what?' Lucas sounded irritated.

'Do you want to talk about what that was like for you?'

'I certainly don't want to. But I think I probably need to. Everything has changed for us. For Rani and me, I mean. It doesn't really feel like there's an *us*, right now.'

'Did he meet little Felix? Do you mind me asking that?'

'Meet him? No way! According to Rani—and I think I actually believe this bit—he doesn't even know the boy exists. Doesn't know he's a biological father. Rani never told him she was pregnant when he left Sydney last time and she still hasn't told him.'

'You mean she hasn't told him she's married with a child?'

'Not sure. I think he knows she's married. I don't know about the child. But she most definitely wouldn't have told him it was *his* child. Oh, you should hear Rani on that subject. *You're the child's father, Lucas—just take a look at his birth certificate!* As if she actually believes it herself.'

Lucas stood up and walked around the room a couple of times. He stopped and looked out the window at a day that was struggling to be sunny. His hands were thrust into his trouser pockets. He turned to Martha. 'You know, the strangest part of all this is that I feel more like the boy's father now than I ever did before. Thanks to dear old Hazel, in a funny way. She's the grandmother he was never going to have.'

'No other grandparents?'

'My parents are both dead. Hadn't I told you that? A light plane crash in North Queensland? Almost four years ago? Just before Felix was born. Her parents are still in India with absolutely no desire to visit. Ever, I'd say. I don't think they've quite forgiven Rani for coming here when she was a student and then deciding to stay. And then actually daring to *marry* an Aussie. Of her *own choice*.'

Lucas paused and turned again to the window. The blossom trees were starting to show their true colours.

'One day, Rani will have to take her son back to see her parents. I doubt if I'll go. I doubt if I'll be invited. Not now, anyway. Not given Rani's new attitude.'

'New attitude to . . .?'

'Oh . . . me. And the boy.'

'You mean since the other Felix's visit?'

'What else would I mean?'

'Do you want to talk about that week? You said you thought you probably needed to . . .'

Lucas sighed. 'Rani went out with him practically every night. Met him straight from work. I did the bedtime routine with the boy on my own.'

'The boy? Don't you want to call him by his name?'

'What do you think?'

'Please go on. I'm sorry I interrupted. I might just keep calling him little Felix, though.'

'The last night he was here she didn't come home at all.'

'That must have been tough for you. Did you know she wouldn't be home?'

'I did. She gave me some cock-and-bull story about a work thing that might go late, it would be easier to stay in town et cetera. She must think I'm an idiot. How long does it take to get home to Artarmon from the city?'

'But she'd told you Felix Kumar was in town.'

'Oh yes. And she was quite open about having dinner with him. She was excited. Couldn't hide it. All dressed up. But I guess admitting she was staying overnight with him would have been a bit too explicit, even for Rani.'

Lucas came away from the window and sat down again.

'Do you know, she hasn't asked to meet Hazel yet? Her own son's carer! Isn't that a bit . . . unusual?'

'It's been a pretty unusual time for you both, by the sound of it. No doubt she'll want to meet Hazel now that things are settling down again.'

'Settling down? What makes you think things are settling down?'

'Sorry. I thought—'

'No, it's okay. I'm just stressed out of my brain. And, to be very frank with you, I'm disturbed by my own reaction. Now her Babu Bangalore has departed our shores, I want Rani more than I ever have before. She's come alive again. Even though I know why, I can't help responding to it. She's back to being Rani the Magnificent. Oh, she's completely untouchable, though. Sorry to use that term. She needs me to keep my feelings to myself. She's in another world. But I badly want to be there with her. Is that weird? Am I crazy?'

'I think you once told me that Rani can be warm and passionate when she wants to be, and rather cold and pragmatic at other times. No doubt she is more attractive to you when she's warmer, even though you have a fair idea about what's warmed her up. You said it yourself—we're complicated creatures, Lucas. Life is complicated. Sometimes our actions take a while to catch up with our feelings. Sometimes our feelings take a while to catch up with our actions.'

Lucas pondered this for a while before responding.

'She's the mother of . . . yeah, let's call him little Felix, although he's already telling me how big he is. *Soon I'll be four*—that's his line. Fed to him by Hazel, no doubt. But, yeah, I'm his dad, more or less. We'll stick together. Rani wants us to stick together as a family. But I wouldn't go through another pregnancy if I knew the baby wasn't mine. I can say that categorically. One of those nights she didn't come home, I achieved great clarity on that point.'

'I can see that. I understand that.'

Another long pause. Another walk to the window.

'That Bill Orton was a lovely chap,' Lucas said, in a completely different tone of voice. Buoyant, almost.

'Oh—Bill. Yes. I saw you two having a good yarn over a glass of Ruby's wine.'

'Hmm. That's a thing I almost forgot. Ruby and Bill both brought wine, and Hazel brought scones, and I came empty-handed. I'm sorry about that. I thought you said not to bring—'

'I did say that. Anyway, you brought little Felix and he was the star of the show.'

'But yeah, no . . . Bill was great. Warm, you know? An open kind of guy. I thought so, anyway. We really connected. Good vibe. He told me a bit about his job. His wife sounds an interesting woman. Difficult, I'd say, from Bill's tone. He asked me a bit about little Felix—you know, looking so Indian and everything. I gave him a version of the truth.'

'A *version* of the truth?'

'Well, just that I was raising him as my own but, as anyone could see . . .'

Martha felt a stab of alarm on Lucas's behalf, but said nothing.

'Yeah, we might reach out to each other again some time,' Lucas said. 'One on one. He's about the same age my dad would've been by now.'

'Lucas, I . . .' Martha hesitated and wished she hadn't opened her mouth.

'What?'

'I'm afraid our time's gone.'

TWENTY-THREE

'SAM? IT'S ME.'

'Oh. Hi, Mum. Nice to hear your voice. How are you getting on? How have you been coping with the fallout from your afternoon tea?'

'Fine. All good, as one of my clients keeps saying. Thanks again for all your help with that. No, there's been some lovely fallout, as you call it.'

'Great. Look, Mum, I'm just about to meet someone. Can I call you back in the morning?'

'Whenever you like. I was really just . . . I know it's breaking all the rules, but I just wondered if there were any developments to report. It can wait till the morning, though.'

'Developments? Oh, you mean Darren. Gosh, that feels like ancient history now. Didn't I tell you what happened? Oh well, his wife copped him preparing the sample. I'll spare you the lurid details. Anyway, he hadn't told her about the deal—*idiot*. So when he owned up, she hit the roof. Not unreasonably, I have to say. End of story. Anyway, I've moved on. So no champagne on your doorstep this month, Mum. Look, sorry, I really do have to dash.'

'Call me in the morning. Earlier the better.'

'Okay. Bye.'

Martha chided herself for having broken her silence on the subject of Darren. She knew Sam would tell her when there was any news to report, but her impatience had, once again, got the better of her. On the other hand, she thought she had detected a new tone in Sam's voice—not excitement, exactly, but something brighter. She knew she was in constant danger of over-interpreting things with Sam, but she still clung to the hope that a new romance might make the quest for a sperm donor redundant.

TWENTY-FOUR

'PHEW. I'M TIRED, DEAR. I'VE BEEN LOOKING FORWARD TO this hour. It's a relief just to sit down. And . . . shoes and socks?'

'By all means, Hazel—off with your shoes. It's good to see you.'

'It's just looking after the boy, of course. Only two days a week. I'd have him every day if I thought I could handle the pace, but, anyway, he needs the company of other children. I'm all in favour of socialisation.'

'Not wearing you out, I hope?'

'Oh, no, no. It's a bit like being back in the classroom. But I do need to build up my fitness a bit. My stamina. That's all. I'm walking more. Which I should have been doing anyway.'

'That all sounds good. Important not to overdo it, though.'

'Don't worry, dear. This body wouldn't let me overdo it even if I wanted to. But the main thing is the preparation. He's a bright little thing, is Felix. Needs to be on the go all day. We sing a lot. We do little craft things, like colouring in and cutting out shapes from paper squares. That's a bit beyond him at present, but he'll get the hang of it. He loves wielding the scissors. I make paper hats for us, which really gets him going. Talk about laugh! I've had to stock up on all this stuff, of course. Story books, too. Endless stories. I found this book about children from all the different nations of the world. You can imagine which page he turns to every single day.'

'Now, Hazel, I do want to hear how things are working out with Felix, but first I want you to close your eyes and just give yourself up to this little massage.'

Hazel did as she was bidden. Martha could hear her breath slowing and watched the expression on Hazel's face relax into something like serenity. The haunted, lonely look had gone.

When they were done, Martha wrapped Hazel's feet in a towel and returned to her chair.

'So,' Martha said, 'quite a revolution in your household.'

'Revolution's the word. This boy has . . . Well, this boy has . . . I'm sorry, dear.' Hazel leaned over and took a tissue from the box kept permanently on Martha's desk. Another trumpet solo. Clive would have been impressed.

'He's transformed your life, Hazel. I can see that.'

'On Monday I'm getting ready for Tuesday, and on Wednesday I'm getting ready for Thursday. I really miss him over the weekend, but I need the rest, dear, let me tell you. I'll tell you another thing that's changed. I just delete those spammy email things. Brandy and Sienna and Crystal and Merrit Bonway—they can email me all they like . . .'

'And that's a relief?'

'Well, I prefer having a real live person to talk to, let's put it that way.'

'Is there anything else on your mind, Hazel? Anything else you'd like to talk about, apart from this *very* good news about little Felix?'

'Oh, don't call him little. No way. *I'm a big boy.* Oh yes.'

'Sorry: Felix! So . . . is there anything else on your mind this week?'

'I've been thinking about that young girl Ruby. She's dying to be a mother. Anyone can see that. I probably spoke out of turn at the afternoon tea—that was lovely, by the way, Martha. I should have said that before. What nice people they all were. But so many of these young things wait until they're too old to really enjoy the experience of having a wee one. I know with Jason—up half the night, nappies, colic and so on. It's not a bed of roses. May I ask . . . did you ever have children yourself?'

'Just the one. A daughter.'

'Lovely. Well, you know what I'm talking about.'

'I do indeed.'

'So do you think that Ruby might be leaving it too late?'

'Look, Hazel, I'm sure you understand that I can't discuss other clients with you. But I'd say Ruby took your advice seriously. I could see she was very attentive.'

'That's good, then.'

'Actually, I have a message for you from Ruby. She loved your scones and wondered if she could have the recipe.'

'Recipe? Goodness me. It's been a long time since I bothered to consult a recipe. I'll try and write it out for her. I'll bring it next time.'

Hazel lapsed into silence, and her face took on a more thoughtful expression.

'Is there something else, Hazel?'

'There is. And you're the only person who'd understand this. Lucas asked me if I could possibly give Felix his bath and get him into his pyjamas before he comes to pick him up. He's been kept late at his work a couple of times, and I've already given Felix his dinner. So I said yes, of course. They only live in Artarmon, so it's a quick trip home to bed for the boy.'

'I hear a "but" . . .'

'I have to confess it disturbed me a bit. Ridiculous, I know. Woman of my age. But the whole bath thing . . .'

'I do understand, Hazel. It's not ridiculous at all. Your age is irrelevant. So how are you managing? I mean, what with having had the bath taken out and everything?'

'As you can imagine, he's too big for the laundry tub. So I bought a little plastic pool type of thing. They call it a splash pool—sort of a cross between a baby bath and a wading pool. I got the delivery man to put it out in the so-called courtyard. Lucas went to Bunnings and got me a very clever hose thing that clips onto the bathroom tap and runs out through the window. So now we have al fresco bathing! Can you believe it? We had the first go last Thursday and Felix thinks it's the greatest thing out. He can splash all he likes. We have bubbles. Plastic ducks, of course. A toy yacht. And I don't feel a bit anxious. It's not like a bath at all.'

'Well done, Hazel. Really. Oh, and don't forget that scone recipe.'

TWENTY-FIVE

IN THE WEEKS FOLLOWING THEIR LUNCH AT OSCAR'S, ROB
and Sam had met for dinner a few times, treading lightly, exploring
the hitherto hidden reaches of each other's lives. They had laughed
at the number of things they had in common, from their love
of wooden rowing boats, butterflies, old Hollywood musicals,
bushwalks and mushroom omelettes to their dislike of dancing
in public, magical realism in fiction, misplaced apostrophes and
all codes of football . . .

One of the most obvious things they had in common was their
connection to Martha, and they both spoke of her with boundless
affection. They acknowledged her as the fixed point around which
all this new excitement had swirled, and laughed at the thought
that, until the magic lunch, they might only have referred to each
other as 'my mother's colleague' and 'my colleague's daughter'.
Now, as they found themselves passing euphorically through the
transition from friendship to the state of being unambiguously and
irrevocably in love, they had occasionally discussed the question
of when they should tell Martha what was happening. Sam was

adamant that their relationship must be kept hidden from her mother for the time being.

'We don't know what she will make of this Rob. She knows that after wasting all those years on a string of hopeless boyfriends, I'm desperate for a baby, and I'd hate for her to think that I had lined you up to be a mere sperm donor. Just another Darren, except in my bed instead of in a specimen jar. And I'd also hate for her to think that you had somehow exploited my rather too obvious vulnerability. No—it's going to be quite confronting for her. Can't we ease her into it?'

Although Rob was happy to go along with her, he didn't share Samantha's reservations. But he knew how protective she was of her mother, and he respected the strength of her conviction.

Even that limited degree of secrecy added a certain piquancy to the early stages of their relationship. Though not exactly clandestine, their time together sometimes felt as if they were a couple of kids hiding their romance from the prying eyes of their parents. And when one of them suggested a particular date—a movie, a gallery, a weekend away in the Hunter Valley—they would routinely raise the question, *Is Martha likely to be there?* Given the gulf between their tastes and hers, and the limitations placed on Martha's mobility by the deteriorating state of her knees, they usually felt safe going wherever they liked.

The process of falling in love had evolved naturally and, it had seemed to them, inevitably. The exciting sense of possibility that had gripped them both over lunch at Oscar's, triggered by Rob's apparently off-handed *maybe* remark, had grown into a thrilling reality.

They had slipped effortlessly into each other's lives. The ten-year age gap had shrunk into insignificance. At every level it seemed they were becoming one, though they talked about becoming three with an eagerness that surprised them both.

Rob rarely mentioned Constancia to Samantha. She had known the name from the several occasions when Martha had fulminated about the damaging effect of Constancia on Rob, and she occasionally saw Rob's face darken, early in their relationship, as he deleted a series of Constancia's texts from his mobile phone, but there were no other signs of her legacy. Samantha had enough history of her own—*I kissed a lot of frogs before I found my prince*, she had once told Rob—to know which questions were better left unasked. All that mattered was that she and Rob had discovered each other in a new way, and were creating their own new world.

Rob had long dreamed of experiencing the kind of love that would make sense of his all-time favourite quote from Plato: *Every heart sings a song, incomplete, until another heart whispers back.* Now his dream had finally come true

TWENTY-SIX

GILES DUBOIS HAD BEEN MUCH ON MARTHA'S MIND. THIS happened to her from time to time. A sudden rush of recollection—steeped in guilt, shame, remorse and perhaps even yearning—that then receded just as suddenly, freeing Martha from the burden of those memories for months or even years at a stretch.

And then it would all come back, as it had now. When memories of Giles revisited her so vividly, Martha sometimes wondered if this could be some form of premonition—was he in danger? Or unwell? In need of some kind of help? Martha was sceptical about the whole idea of premonitions, though she had worked with several clients who claimed to have experienced vivid telepathic vibes. In her own case, she preferred to think that she was simply being swept back and forth by the tides of wistfulness and regret. Or perhaps merely responding to the human urge to make sense of what's happened to us by facing up to even the most painful parts of our story.

There were consolations in these recollections of her time with Giles, though. When she heard clients recount their complicated, bittersweet love stories—often believing they'd found perfection and then discovering they hadn't—Martha liked to remind herself that she had been there too. She knew what it felt like. She hadn't missed out. She herself did once have a great love, and it wasn't Simon.

Though the memory of it sometimes made her feel foolish, she really did feel in the beginning as if Giles Dubois had been an angel: *A fallen angel, to be sure, but which of us isn't?* He was the only man she had ever given herself to without reservation. The only man—the only person—she had ever felt able to trust with her secret about Sam's conception.

Even ten years later, Martha was able to recall with complete clarity the day—the moment—Giles entered her life. He was booked for a five o'clock appointment on a Friday, and when he walked through her door, before he had uttered a word, Martha fell under a kind of spell. The room seemed filled with light. When Giles shook her hand, she felt an electric charge go through her. Her knees actually trembled. She quickly invited him to sit down, so she could sit too.

The details of that first consultation had remained with her. Looking back, she realised they should have served as a warning. Giles had told her about his struggle with depression 'and a few other things'—unspecified—and said he was seeing a psychiatrist. But he had wanted to impress on Martha that his reason for coming to see her was not . . . he used the word 'clinical'. It was not clinical. He had said he felt purposeless, rudderless, unfulfilled. Martha was particularly struck by his mention of 'existential despair'. Yet his description of his condition was so fluent, so clear, so confident, it was hard for Martha to reconcile the way he presented himself with the way he claimed to be feeling.

At that first session, he had talked incessantly, and Martha was mesmerised. He went on at great length about his love of music, Haydn in particular. His love of reading—he claimed to have devoured both Joyce and Proust, which impressed Martha, since she had tried and abandoned both. He mentioned that he wrote poetry—for therapy, he said, but when Martha later saw his work, she believed she had caught a glimpse of a true poet in his ability to distil a world into a word. She had kept the only poem he ever wrote for her.

He stood erect and looked solid and strong. He had intense brown eyes and long, dark, wavy hair. He had a quick, almost tentative smile that Martha found utterly engaging. His voice was deep and mellifluous, with still a hint of the accent he had brought with him from Belgium when he migrated with his parents to Australia as a schoolboy.

Being constantly distracted by the sound of his voice and that hair curling around his collar, Martha struggled to pay attention to what Giles was saying. But she did calm down enough to realise that Giles was a damaged, troubled man who badly needed help. As his story unfolded, then and at subsequent sessions, Martha felt as if this was the moment she had trained for, dreamed of, worked towards. The care of souls? Here, she thought, was a soul reaching out, crying out, for some care.

From that very first encounter, Martha had felt herself caught in a maelstrom of conflicting emotions. How badly she wanted to be part of the healing process for this man! And . . . and . . . and how badly she wanted this man!

At their first session, six o'clock came and went, but the talking continued. Sandrine had tapped on the door and asked if it was alright for her to leave, and Martha knew that was Sandrine's diplomatic way of offering Martha the chance to extract herself from a difficult situation, if that's what it had become. But Martha had simply smiled reassuringly. Sandrine had frowned as she closed the door and withdrew.

By seven o'clock, Martha had become ravenous, so she smiled and said, 'I need something to eat.' She had tried to couch it in terms that wouldn't sound like an explicit invitation that might have made Giles feel awkward. But when she had said she was going to a nearby cafe, he had unhesitatingly said he would join her. It had seemed so easy and natural then. *Everything* had seemed easy and natural in those early weeks. They walked to a little cafe in Archer Street and had what Martha later described to one of her friends as 'a simple meal and a complex conversation'. In Martha's memory, that conversation had been deep, expansive, intriguing . . . a torrent of words had poured forth from Giles, though she could never recall much of what had actually been said. She did remember thinking that she was speaking less than she normally would in a social situation. But by ten o'clock, she no longer knew whether this was a social situation, an extended consultation, a seduction, or a train wreck.

The cafe shut at ten, and they walked back to the cottage together, where they bid each other goodnight and shook hands.

By the next morning, Martha was feeling grateful that their first meeting had been on a Friday night, because she had been unable to sleep. On that Saturday, she almost laughed at herself for being trapped in a cliché, but she really had not slept a wink. She had never lost a night's sleep over Simon, even when they were teenagers. She was smitten in a way that seemed utterly beyond her control. She felt as if she had been dumped in the surf, and wasn't enjoying it any more than she enjoyed actually being dumped in the surf. She would later recall those early weeks as being distressing, disorientating and destabilising . . . and blissful.

Saturday was generally Martha's recovery day. She liked to spend it adrift with the weekend papers, a bit of radio, and a late-afternoon walk. She sometimes met a friend for coffee or a drink. But it was downtime. Her time. R and R. But that particular Saturday had simply passed in a blur of emotional confusion.

Martha saw Giles again the following Friday at the same time. Sandrine had enquired, in her gentle way, about that first session, and Martha had lied about how long it had lasted, and what had followed. She had approached their second session with such anxiety that she had several times pretended to herself she was considering cancelling it.

He came again. He talked again. At ten to six he looked at his watch and said, 'I mustn't keep you talking.' He rose to leave, and Martha panicked.

As they stood together inside Martha's office door, Giles said, 'I wonder if we might plan another conversation away from here. I don't wish to break the rules. Shall I give you my mobile number? Please call me if you'd like to arrange to meet at another time, perhaps for coffee.'

He handed Martha his card (embossed, classy, restrained—just his name and a mobile number) and left without another word. She later came to feel that was typical of him: leaving it up to her to take the initiative. At the time, she just thought he was being discreet.

As though propelled by an irresistible force, and with a sense of the utter inevitability of what would follow, Martha rang him, they met for coffee, and then, a few days later, for a meal. The frequency of their private meetings steadily increased, but they kept their Friday counselling appointments, as well. It felt to Martha as if they were trying to occupy two different worlds simultaneously.

That lasted for four weeks. They both realised it was an unsustainable situation. Martha, for her part, knew she had already trashed her code of professional conduct, even without going to bed with Giles—though she knew that would happen soon enough.

Even before the relationship became sexual, Martha felt that she had completely surrendered herself to Giles—to the idea of her and Giles as a couple. She had experienced anxiety, but no guilt, about their evolving situation, even though she knew her behaviour would not be condoned by anyone else. From the moment they began sleeping together, Martha had been wondering—planning—how to extricate herself from the glaringly obvious conflict of interest. But the issue was never how to bring the personal relationship with Giles to an end; rather, she had become preoccupied with the possibility of stepping away from her professional practice and devoting herself to an entirely new life with Giles.

The first step in that process had been easy to manage. She simply stopped seeing Giles as a client. She tried to convince herself that their relationship had moved irrevocably from the professional to the exclusively personal, though that turned out to be a gross over-simplification. For all their time together, and especially towards the end, Martha continued to try to care for that deeply troubled, deeply needy soul. Her devotion to Giles had started as a passion and become a mission.

Martha had just turned fifty-seven when she met Giles, so the idea that she might take a year off for some overseas travel—or even decide to retire completely—did not seem odd. Giles was ten years younger than Martha, so he had many working years ahead of him, though his parents had left him rather well off, and he had once remarked to Martha that he didn't really need to work, and didn't enjoy the kind of work he was doing. (She never established precisely what that was, though he had once rather vaguely said he was 'between assignments' for a company that organised trade fairs and conventions.)

Their escape strategy was entirely conceived by Martha. The plan was to leave Sydney and travel for a year in Europe, using Giles's original home town, Brussels, as their base. Making their travel plans was a breeze. Giles simply left all the arrangements to Martha. She knew he was still seeing his psychiatrist regularly, still taking his medication, and she assumed that might account for his acquiescence. He occasionally showed signs of anxiety about the idea of a long-haul flight, but Martha found it easy to convince him that all would be well once they arrived in Brussels and began their new life together. Later, she had to admit—to herself, and to a therapist she was then seeing—that she had no idea of the extent of Giles's mental health issues. He had assured her there was no problem about being away for so long—his psychiatrist would supply the necessary medication and prescriptions, and she had also given him the name of a colleague based in Brussels in case he needed on-the-spot help.

All Martha told Rob was that she was planning some overseas travel with a new man in her life, and would need time out from the practice. She said nothing about how Giles and she had met. Rob had said he was delighted that Martha was contemplating such an adventure. He wanted to meet Giles, but Martha resisted that and was glad, later, that she had. She and Rob agreed that a part-time locum would be employed for the year Martha planned to be away, and Rob had quickly found a suitable person—a young psychologist he knew called Zoe who was keen to take it on.

Sandrine, the soul of discretion, had obviously connected the dots but never uttered a tactless word.

Sam was getting on with her own life and seemed relaxed about her mother's change of direction. Barely thirty, she had already launched her interior design business, which was beginning to prosper. She had what she described to Martha as a 'promising' boyfriend on the scene—though he turned out to be all promise and no delivery. She met Giles only once before he and Martha left for Europe, and seemed to like him. She was too distracted to realise what an upheaval this was for her mother, though she did once say, over the phone to Martha, 'I hope you know what you're doing.'

Martha's two closest friends met Giles over breakfast and were enchanted, as most people were on their first meeting with him. One of them, recently divorced, had asked Martha to let her know if the relationship didn't work out and Giles came back on the market.

Their departure from Sydney went smoothly, helped along by Martha's conviction that she was about to start a new life with the man of her dreams, though she had assured Giles that she had never dared to dream of anyone quite as wonderful as he was.

After their return from Europe, Martha had reflected on the trip in her journal: *To say it seemed like a good idea at the time would be vacuous. Of course it seemed like a good idea at the time. At the time, it seemed like the fulfilment of destiny.*

Only later did it occur to me that I knew almost nothing about Giles apart from his opinions. I had no appreciation, in the beginning, of the extent of his psychosis or the depth of his delusions. I should have been alert to the signs. I knew he was wounded, but I saw myself as his healer. Pride goeth before a fall. I should have remembered that.

TWENTY-SEVEN

MORE THAN A MONTH HAD PASSED SINCE BILL HAD TURNED up late to the client afternoon tea, and Martha had begun to wonder if she would ever see the Ortons again as a couple. Based on their two sessions with her, Martha had thought Abigail an unlikely candidate for psychotherapy, lacking any apparent appetite for self-examination. And Bill? He had struck Martha as a pleasant fellow, warm, well meaning, though rather defensive, as if he felt he was in constant danger of being outmanoeuvred by his wife. They had seemed an unlikely couple but, then, so did many other couples Martha saw. The difference, in the Ortons' case, was Martha's nagging doubt about the authenticity of their presentation.

As the weeks had gone by, part of her had been relieved by the thought that she might never again have to endure Abigail's aggression and volatility. But when Sandrine announced that she'd made a third appointment for the Ortons, Martha found she was looking forward to having another opportunity to crack the Orton code. The idea that Bill's spine might need stiffening had always sounded to Martha like the flimsiest of pretexts for their sessions with her. Something was seriously awry in their marriage, she felt sure, but so far they'd managed to keep their secret hidden from her. Was it still hidden from them, too? That was what she needed to discover.

Her professional spirit was sustained by revelations and clarifications; by helping her clients find a way to lift the veil of obfuscation from the stories they were telling themselves. Usually, clients were unaware of the veil's existence, but in the Ortons' case . . .

From the moment they came in and sat down, Martha sensed a radical shift in the dynamic. Abigail now exuded a calm confidence—more assured and less edgy than before—whereas Bill looked as if he were discharging an obligation, like a reluctant churchgoer.

'Good morning to you both,' Martha said, maintaining as light a tone as she could muster.

'Is it, though?' Abigail replied, immediately on the front foot. '*Is* it a good morning?'

'It was just a manner of speaking, Abigail. A greeting.'

Bill glared at his wife, as if appealing to her to desist.

'It looks like a good morning for you, anyway,' Abigail said. 'You're very nicely set up here. Very comfortable. Good flow of clients. We found it quite hard to get this third appointment. Booked out, is that right?'

'Abigail, I don't think it's helpful to discuss the state of my appointment book. Is there something else you'd like to talk about this morning? *Either* of you?' Martha looked expectantly at Bill.

'Yes, Martha,' he said. 'This is not a counselling matter, I realise, but I did want to thank you for that very pleasant little occasion a few weeks back. I apologise again for my late arrival. There was a misunderstanding about the arrangements.'

'Not at all, Bill. I know the others enjoyed meeting you.'

'Yes, well, I just wanted to say that.'

I just wanted to say that. Martha read a kind of warning in Bill's tone, as if he wanted to observe the normal courtesies before the unpleasantness began. He looked distinctly uneasy and kept glancing sideways at Abigail.

'It must feel like a pretty secure existence for you, Martha,' Abigail said. 'I mean, you sit in here, playing God with people's lives, never giving away a thing about your own. People look to you to help them wrestle with their moral issues, I have no doubt. Oh, I have *no* doubt. And you sit there and listen and try to look oh-so-pure and undefiled. No flies on Martha. *Ha.*'

'Abigail, I'm not sure what this is about, but I assure you the problems I try to help my clients deal with are not moral problems, as such. There will sometimes be a moral dimension, I grant you. But I'm a psychologist, as you well know, not a moral philosopher. I try to help my clients to recover their emotional equilibrium, mostly. I'm realistic about what can be achieved. And I can also assure you I don't adopt a superior moral position. Ever. We touched on that last time. But I really don't want to go over this again, Abigail. I'd like you to tell me what's been on your mind—it's quite a while since you were here. Last time, weren't we talking about your wish for Bill to be a little more assertive in the marriage?'

'Leave Bill out of this, okay?'

Bill leaned forward as if he might be about to speak, but he didn't.

'So,' Abigail said, 'not a moral philosopher. But you wanted to be, didn't you? Wasn't that your first love?'

Martha frowned. She had mentioned, in passing, her initial enthusiasm for philosophy to Lucas—that was possibly a mistake—but she was certain she'd never mentioned it to the Ortons. Why would she? And would Lucas have mentioned it to Bill when they were chatting over a drink on that Saturday afternoon? Unlikely, surely. And what was Abigail's point, anyway? Was this intended as a fresh line of attack on Martha's professional integrity?

'Abigail, I'm sure we could have a lovely time reminiscing about what we did and didn't enjoy when we were students. But I really must ask you to move off this concern with my situation, my circumstances. Can we get to the reason you're here?'

'Ah, but you *are* the reason we're here.'

'Me? In what sense, Abigail? I assume you're here because I'm a counsellor, but I have to be frank with you: there are obvious matters needing attention. You've said so yourself. But—'

'Obvious matters? What *obvious* matters?'

Again, Martha turned towards Bill for support, but his eyes were downcast and he looked as if he would rather be anywhere but there.

'It's not up to me to—'

'Oh, do I detect a whiff of hypocrisy? The very thing I told you I can't stand! Didn't I tell you that? On our very first visit? Or have you forgotten? Let's hear it. What matters do you think need attending to? You think we're in need of some sort of marriage guidance. Is that it?'

'I thought you indicated that was the case, yes. And I must ask you to moderate your tone, Abigail. We won't be able to proceed if we can't speak respectfully to each other.'

'But what if we *don't* respect each other? Should we still speak respectfully? Wouldn't that be yet another case of hypocrisy?'

'*Abby!*' Bill had risen to his feet and was positioning himself in front of his wife with his back to Martha, as if forming a shield between them. 'You've gone too far,' he hissed. 'This is an outrage, and I won't be part of it. I'm not going to sit by and listen to you harass this woman for no reason at all. What has she ever done to you?'

A tense silence filled the space. No one moved. Martha's mind was racing, racing, trying to locate some kernel of meaning in what Abigail was saying. Some way of making sense of it. Something to work with. Some way to unfreeze the moment.

It was Abigail who spoke first.

'Bill, sit down and be quiet, or else remove your person.'

'I'm not going anywhere.'

'Then sit down.'

Bill hesitated. He turned to face Martha and she nodded at him. He returned to his chair.

'Hypocrisy? Let's start with this one. How many clients have you slept with, Martha? How many of your clients realise you could have been—*should* have been—deregistered for breaking your professional code? You shouldn't still be allowed to practice. You know that and I know that. You're just dead lucky no one reported you, aren't you? *Aren't you,* Martha? What if someone reported you now? What if *I* reported you? It's not too late. I checked the healthcare complaints website. Would you like to know what it says? I'm sure you've checked it very carefully yourself. *Very* carefully, I imagine.'

Martha felt her face flushing. She had an uneasy sense of where this might be leading, and she had no desire to pursue it. 'Abigail, I really must ask you to leave. Now, please.'

Bill stood. Abigail remained defiantly seated.

'I'm not going anywhere just yet. I won't be coming back. But I'm paying for this session and you can hear me out. There are some unresolved matters—some injustices—that have dragged on for far too long. Some wrongs that need to be righted.'

Martha was now deeply disturbed by Abigail's increasingly strident tone. She realised it was entirely possible that Abigail might have known someone who knew about Martha's affair with Giles. But that was a ten-year-old story. Giles had never lodged a complaint—why would he?—and Martha had left the practice for twelve months. That had been her way of acknowledging that she had done the wrong thing, almost like self-imposed penance.

But why now? What possible motive could Abigail have for bringing this up? The woman was dangerous, that much was clear. Nothing else was.

'I have a twin sister called Gabrielle. Does that name ring a bell?'

Martha shook her head, willing Abigail to finish quickly and leave. Why should the name of Abigail's sister be of any interest to her?

'Let me tell you a bit about Gabrielle. We're very close, like a lot of identical twins. As a matter of fact, *close* doesn't begin to describe it. We really are like two halves of one person. That's how we started, after all—one egg split into two halves—and that's how we've always been. If something happens to Gabby— Gabrielle—I feel as if it's happening to me, and vice versa. I'll give you an example. When we were in our twenties, Gabrielle was injured in a car crash when she was on holiday in Queensland. I felt it. I mean, I actually felt as if I'd been struck. I called her to see if she was okay and, sure enough, she'd been injured and was briefly in emergency.'

Abigail paused and looked to Martha for a response. Martha nodded. All she wanted was for this to be over.

'A lot of the time,' Abigail went on, 'we know what the other one is thinking, even when we're not together. For us, it's never been a matter of having a sister—it's literally been like having our other half. When we were growing up, we shared all our clothes—there was never "hers" and "mine", only "ours". Even our shoes. Even our undies. You probably think I'm exaggerating, Martha. You probably think that sounds weird.'

Martha was becoming increasingly perplexed by Abigail's story; increasingly impatient; increasingly frustrated.

'Not at all, Abigail. I've read the research on identical twins. Some of them do feel pretty much the way you've described your relationship with your own sister. So, not weird, no. But yours is certainly an extreme manifestation of the twin experience, I'd say.'

Martha was alarmed by the tone of pomposity in her own voice.

'Would you now? An extreme manifestation! Is that what you'd say? Well, it doesn't feel extreme to us. It's just the way it's always been. Everyone called us Abby and Gabby, by the way. Our parents had a sense of humour, see, unlike some others in this room. When we were young, people literally couldn't tell us apart. We once tricked Bill on a date—Gabby pretended to be me. Remember that, Bill? Don't worry; she only let him go as far as I was letting him go at the time. Anyway, as I said, we're really like one person in two halves. Not just close—*connected*. I'll tell you something else that will probably interest a person like you, Martha. Bill doesn't like Gabby at all—can't stand her, actually, even though I'd say she's a bit softer around the edges than I am—so that tells you something rather significant, doesn't it?'

Bill glared at his wife. 'Abby, I don't think—'

Abigail held up her hand to silence him. 'Anyway, I'll come to the point. Fisher was our family name, so we used to be Abby and Gabby Fisher. Then we had a very lavish double wedding—identical wedding dresses, of course, and two bridesmaids apiece, all in identical kit. I married a man called Orton and Gabby married a man called Watson. Pretty standard English names, aren't they? All three of them. Fisher. Orton. Watson. Perfectly ordinary names.'

Abigail paused and examined her fingernails. Martha said nothing.

'The marriage to Watson lasted quite a long time, Martha. Two gorgeous children. They're my nieces, of course, but they practically feel like my own daughters, especially as Bill and I have no kids of our own. But back to Mr Watson. He turned out to be a rogue and they eventually split up. Gabby was devastated. And so was I, of course. *Devastated.* I told you we feel everything together. But guess what happened next, Martha?'

'How could I possibly know what happened next?'

'Well, things took an unexpected turn for the better. Gabby met a lovely, lovely man who had been badly wounded by a previous relationship. He had been very shabbily treated indeed. Disgracefully treated, I'd say. And when my own dear Gabby got caught up in this man's situation, well, so did I, just as if it was happening to me, too. So I watched my poor sister wrestle with the thought that this beautiful new man in her life was so damaged, he might never heal. He sees a therapist twice a week. Imagine that—*twice a week*. Just to be able to function. Naturally, Gabby and I share the load—she takes him on Tuesdays and I do the Friday run. He and I chat away as if . . . well, you can imagine. There are no secrets.'

Martha was beginning to experience some difficulty in breathing, but she continued looking steadily at Abigail.

'Anyway,' Abigail went on, 'the thing is that in spite of all the obvious questions about his mental health, Gabby loved him—we *both* loved him—and she recently decided to marry him. Isn't that wonderful? She has become Mrs Dubois. *Martha?* Are you listening to me?'

Martha was rigid in her seat. Shocked beyond speech. At last she knew where this had been heading all along.

Abigail wasn't finished. 'So now Gabby and I know lots of things about Martha Elliott that other people don't know. *Lots* of things. Things that not even her own daughter knows. *Not even her own daughter*, Martha. Samantha Elliott, that high-profile interior designer. Didn't I read recently that she won some award? Was that her? There was even a picture of the interior of her home in . . . Crows Nest, I think. Is that right?'

Abigail paused to let this sink in, watching Martha with the intensity of a bird of prey.

After a moment, she went on: 'Meanwhile, poor Giles Dubois is really struggling to get on with his new life. I thought you'd like to know that, seeing you're doing so well with your own cosy little life.'

Martha sat motionless as Abigail and Bill got up to go. Abigail headed straight for the door. Bill paused in front of Martha. 'I'm sorry,' he said. 'I've tended to stay clear of this Giles chap. He seems a bit odd, frankly, but I honestly have no idea what Abby is on about. I think I might need to come and see you on my own.'

Martha remained immobile for several minutes after the Ortons' departure, breathing deeply and trying to compose herself. Shocking enough was the revelation that Abigail Orton, of all people, was so close to Giles. Even more shocking was that explicit mention of 'things that not even her own daughter knows'. There was little doubt—*no* doubt, surely—that this was a reference to Sam's biological father. The one confidence Martha had felt sure Giles would never betray.

A friend of Martha's was fond of quoting an American expression about consequences: *If you didn't want to go to Chicago, you shouldn't have got on the train.* Well, here we are in Chicago, Martha said to herself. Took a while to get here. What now?

She walked into the reception area and asked Sandrine if Rob was free.

'He's booked solid today, Martha. Not even a proper lunch break. I'm going to nip over to Oscar's and get him a sandwich.'

'Let me do it,' Martha said. 'I feel like some fresh air.'

'Are you sure? Roast beef, egg and onion. Multigrain. Untoasted.'

'Okay. What have I got on this afternoon?'

'You're pretty free. Only Ruby at five.'

'Could you see if you can move her to tomorrow, please? Or Monday? I think I'll take the rest of the day off.'

'Are you okay, Martha?'

'Okay? Not really. But I'll be fine. I just need to clear my head. I'll go and get Rob's sandwich. Do you want anything?'

'No, I'll go out later. Are you sure you're okay? You look a bit . . . shook.'

'Shook is the perfect word, Sandy. *Shook.* That's exactly what I am.'

'Anything I can do to help?'

'Just go right on being the dear Sandrine you've always been. That's the most helpful thing you can do for me, right now. My very own Rock of Gibraltar.'

Sandrine smiled at the compliment, but seemed embarrassed. 'They're a strange pair, the Ortons,' she said quickly. 'He seems quite a nice man, but I can't warm to her at all. Sorry. I know you don't like me commenting on clients.'

'Did they happen to pay this time?'

'They did.'

'Ah.'

'Are we expecting them to make another appointment?'

'No, Sandy. They won't be coming back.'

⁓

Hi Gabs

Nearly there. Lowered the boom today. She knows we know. Boy is she one creepy lady. Talk about stitched up. But I think she was rattled. Finally. Will you tell Giles yet?

Abs xox

> *Brave girl, Abs. I'll keep Himself in the dark a tad longer. Bit unsteady at the mo. Unpredictable, except for you know what. Wait till we're sure the witch is totally sidelined. No more danger to the paying public. Call me asap.*
>
> *Gabs xox*

TWENTY-EIGHT

MARTHA HAD FLOWN STRAIGHT TO BRUSSELS WITH GILES. It was her first time in Europe and she was enchanted from the moment they arrived. They checked into the Hotel le Châtelain and enjoyed a week of being pampered before finding a small apartment they could afford to rent, in a charmless concrete block that contrasted sharply with the architectural splendours of the city. Their first and, as it turned out, their only home together.

Ten years on, Martha still recalled those early weeks in Brussels as one of the most exquisite periods of her life. Being with Giles was everything she had hoped it would be.

They decided to stay in Brussels for a while, only travelling as far as nearby towns and villages for short visits. Antwerp, Bruges, Waterloo . . . All charming, beautiful, historic places, but Martha felt as if she were seeing everything through a haze of desire. Giles needed to make love to her every day, sometimes twice in a day. At first, that seemed very flattering to her—she had never previously been desired like that, though she had cause to reflect rather wryly that her post-menopausal body was not as eager or responsive as it might once have been.

But then, after only a few weeks of what had felt like unalloyed bliss, Martha began to sense that something was seriously wrong. For a start, she found herself resenting all that sex. Even dreading it. The relentlessness of it. It was almost as if sex was just part of some therapeutic regimen that kept Giles on a reasonably even keel. It was coming to seem less about Martha, or even about them as a couple, and more about Giles and his own needs.

Martha had previously regarded physical intimacy as the ultimate symbol of emotional intimacy—although that hadn't turned out to be true with Simon. But Giles soon cured her of that romantic notion. In the beginning, though, she really did feel more intensely desired, more alive, than she ever had, before or since.

Giles was not only relentless about sex; he was also a relentless talker. Although Martha did her best to keep listening, she sometimes felt in desperate need of a break.

Before long, the initial excitement about being in such a spectacular, stimulating place with Giles began to lose its sheen. By their fourth week in Brussels, Martha was struggling to come to terms with the fact that Giles was a far more deeply troubled man than she had previously acknowledged. While she still felt devoted to him—possibly even more than before, as his assorted frailties, phobias and neuroses became more obvious—she was now facing the tricky prospect of trying to reconcile the roles of carer and lover.

She had initially assumed that Giles was keen to stay in Brussels as a way of settling into their new life together—they had never actually lived together in Sydney and so they were adapting to each other in the subtle and awkward ways of old-fashioned newlyweds. But she gradually came to realise that, although they had flown halfway around the world to get there, Giles was curiously reluctant to plan any travel beyond Belgium's borders. He actually seemed terrified by the prospect, as if he were suffering from a kind of selective agoraphobia.

Martha was initially amused, and then alarmed to find that his lachanophobia—fear of vegetables—was also highly selective, being confined to broccoli. There was nothing selective about his claustrophobia, though—whenever they were indoors, Giles took great care to position himself near an exit or an open window.

He was also terrified of heights. He couldn't bear to be any higher than a first-floor balcony. Their visit to Waterloo was marred by a panic attack he suffered when Martha suggested they climb to the top of Lion's Mound to view the battlefield. Giles wouldn't set foot on even the bottom step, as if he were afraid that Martha might try to persuade him to keep climbing.

He feared strangers, too. He resisted all Martha's suggestions that they should make an effort to meet their neighbours in the apartment block. He let Martha make all the personal connections with local shopkeepers, though his French was fluent and hers was strictly schoolgirl.

Considering that Giles's family was Belgian, Martha had assumed there would be relatives to meet. In fact, she had been looking forward to being introduced as his partner. No such contacts were ever made. Giles acknowledged there were cousins he had known as a child, but he showed no interest in reconnecting with them. He had seemed irritated when Martha first raised this, soon after their arrival, and became positively angry when she dared to mention it once or twice later. In fact, anger became an increasingly common feature of Giles's behaviour towards her.

After their first month in Brussels, Giles began to criticise Martha for all kinds of things he had never previously objected to.

He might say, 'When you walk with me in public, please stand up straighter. And don't sway from side to side like that.' Or, 'Your jaw clicks when you eat. It's so loud I'm embarrassed to eat with you in public.' (In fact, Martha's jaw did click when she ate, and she had always been a bit self-conscious about it.) Or he'd say something like, 'Why don't you dress more stylishly—look how elegant these European women are.'

At first, Martha tried to laugh these criticisms off, as if Giles couldn't be serious. As time passed, though, she came to regard them as rather distressing symptoms of Giles's own insecurities and anxieties, projected onto her. That interpretation made them a little easier for her to bear, though there were times when she couldn't restrain herself from snapping at him in response, which only provoked more anger.

In spite of all that, Martha still found much about Giles that she loved, or wanted to love. And she kept trying to find ways to make him happy, even though she would have bristled if a client had said that about someone in their life.

Quite early in their stay, it dawned on Martha that what she had previously thought of as Giles's deferential, sensitive approach to decision-making was actually a sign of his inability to decide anything. As time went by, she found she was deciding absolutely everything—from the destination of their next daytrip to what clothes Giles should wear, and where and what they would eat.

Coming from Australia, Martha could hardly believe how close they were by rail to some of the world's most attractive cities. An hour and a half to Paris! Two hours to Amsterdam! And, thanks to her gentle but persistent persuasion, they did manage a few excursions. Austria was the only country Giles was actually keen to visit, being the home of his beloved Joseph Haydn. They spent three weekends in Vienna, always for concerts. By then, Martha had had her fill of Haydn, though she didn't dare say so.

Whenever they were in Brussels, daily visits to the Grand-Place were so doggedly, obsessively insisted on by Giles that Martha finally became desensitised to its grandeur. Equally obsessive was the ritual of their daily homage to Manneken-Pis, the bronze statue of a little boy relieving himself that seemed to amuse Giles afresh, each time he saw it.

There were many lovely moments that would always remain precious in Martha's memory, but, as time passed, they became less frequent and less lovely. Giles's moods needed constant monitoring. And Martha soon came to understand why he had been seeing his psychiatrist weekly. She was feeling increasingly foolish—and increasingly remorseful—about her failure to have fully processed the significance of that before they left Sydney. 'I was almost literally blinded by passion' was her attempt to justify it later. Martha had tried to persuade Giles to see the Brussels psychiatrist he'd been referred to, but he refused to seek medical help of any kind. He had stockpiled a supply of Xanax that he became increasingly reliant on. There were days when he was so heavily sedated, he seemed almost like a zombie. Though she hated to admit it to herself, Martha found those days easier to handle. She had finally come to accept that her challenge was to hold Giles together until she could get him safely back home to Sydney.

During their final weeks in Brussels, Martha had established regular email contact with Rob and was also able to speak to him by phone at times when Giles was in a drugged sleep. Rob had been sympathetic, but Martha had trouble convincing him that her resources as a carer were exhausted and that she was even starting to doubt her capacity to manage the journey home.

Rob had finally agreed to contact Giles's psychiatrist and she managed to secure a place for him in a private psychiatric clinic in Neutral Bay where, she told Rob, Giles had previously spent some time. (That was yet another thing Martha had not known about Giles.)

After barely three months, the return to Sydney had become an urgent necessity, for Giles's health and wellbeing and for Martha's. Their dream—perhaps it had only ever really been Martha's dream— of an exciting new life together was in tatters.

TWENTY-NINE

'IS THIS A GOOD MOMENT, ROB?'

It was late on Friday afternoon. Martha had taken the rest of Thursday off to recover from her final encounter with the Ortons, and to gather her thoughts. Sandrine had moved Ruby's appointment to the following Monday. So Friday had been a free day for Martha, too, and Rob had not expected her to come in for a Life and Times session. But here she was.

'Grab a pew, Martha,' Rob said, looking intently at her. 'A rough time?'

'You could say that.'

'Sandrine said you'd been shaken up by that pair, so I thought I'd leave you in peace. Thanks for buying my lunch, by the way.'

'Pleasure. I really need to talk to you about the Ortons. I've brought a bottle. Will you open it?'

Rob went to the kitchen and brought back two glasses, opened and poured the wine and settled back into his chair. His had also been a difficult week, in its own way, thanks to Constancia. After weeks of silence, she had taken to peppering him with angry,

183

pleading and abusive texts and voicemail messages. He had finally decided to block her number, but this was clearly not the moment to discuss that with Martha. And Samantha was still postponing the moment when they might tell Martha about their relationship.

'There has been what you might call a development. Taking us—me—back ten years,' Martha said, after they had proposed their ritual toast to mental health, including each other's.

'Oh?'

'You can't guess?'

'Ten years ago . . . Wasn't that when you took your aborted Euro-sabbatical with Monsieur Dubois? Can't see the link.'

'Giles has recently married.'

'Well, that's good news. I mean . . . it is, isn't it? Sounds as if he's well and truly back in the saddle, so to speak. You're not going to tell me you're still carrying a torch for that guy.'

'Certainly not. Not at all. No way.' Martha heard herself issue those three denials and wondered if, even now, there was a vestige of the Giles effect still in her system. Surely not.

'So what's the problem?'

'He's married the twin sister of our very own Abigail Orton.'

'Wow, what a coincidence! Small world and all that.'

'Not a coincidence at all. She was only pretending to be a client. Doing her sister's dirty work for her. Initially just trying to tease me. Undermine me. Maybe just puzzle me. Destabilise me, anyway. It hadn't really worked, until yesterday. Let me tell you as much of this murky story as you absolutely need to know. That much and no more.'

'Ugly?'

'Very.'

Rob saw a shadow cross Martha's face, as if she were being revisited by the pain of that long-ago heartbreak. All the grief and despair that Rob had observed but never quite understood. He vividly remembered her retreat into a period of terrible self-neglect. She had put on weight, let her hair grow and seemed to have lost all interest in her personal appearance. When she'd returned to work a few months later, her appearance had improved, but the ravages of the Dubois episode had never quite left her face or her figure.

'I'm listening. Take it easy, Martha.'

'No, I'm okay. It's just that this has dug up some very old stuff that I'd been hoping to leave buried. I never told you this, but Giles was originally a client.'

Martha looked at Rob, expecting . . . what? Shock? Outrage? Displeasure, at least. But there was nothing.

'Tell me something I didn't know,' was all he said.

'How . . .?'

'Martha, his name was in the appointment book. In the accounts. There aren't a lot of Giles Duboises about. Were you really so blinded by infatuation that you thought I wouldn't twig?'

'Didn't you disapprove?'

'Disapprove? Yeah, I guess. Wildly unethical. But I also thought it was none of my business. And I admired your strategy for dealing with it.'

Martha smiled at him. She disapproved—that probably *was* the right word—of his relationship with Constancia, even though it was not 'wildly unethical'. It was just damaging. Corrosive. How could Rob not see that?

'I notice you used the word infatuation. Wasn't that a bit unkind, Rob? I loved that man with all of my being. I'm serious.'

'Well, I seem to recall you went pretty close to mocking me when I spoke of how devoted I was to . . . to Constancia.'

Martha noticed the hesitation, the catch in Rob's voice. She also noted Rob's use of the past tense, but said nothing.

'Okay,' Rob said. 'No point-scoring. Fair enough. I shouldn't have said infatuation. One person's infatuation is another's grand passion. We know that. Let's just say you were cognitively impaired. Is that better? Not a bad description of being in love, is it?'

Martha failed to raise a smile.

'Anyway,' she said, 'the point is that Abigail issued a not-very-veiled threat to report me to the complaints tribunal. I can't say I think it's likely to happen, and I'm by no means sure it would be taken seriously, given all the circumstances and the time that's elapsed. But . . .'

Rob nodded. 'But, indeed. These things are very unpredictable.'

'I could pre-empt them. I could go talk to someone. But I'm loath to do that. I don't want to go through the humiliation of trawling through all that history if I don't have to. I'd feel a complete dope if Abigail or her sister—or Giles—never actually followed through.'

'Quite. But I'd support you, if it came to that, Martha. You know I would.'

'Thanks for saying that, Rob. But—'

'Sorry to interrupt, but I have to ask you: did you ever do the foot thing with the Ortons?'

'I don't like the dismissive way you say *the foot thing*, Rob. This is a serious therapeutic treatment. Not trivial. Not just a *thing*, as you so unkindly put it. But no, I never offered it to them. It never seemed appropriate. Why do you ask?'

'Probably just as well. Look, Martha, I know you're touchy about this, but . . . well, we both know someone could dob you in for mixing that up with counselling sessions. I mean, from a registration point of view. It's your own business, of course. It's just that I have sometimes wondered if it made you a bit vulnerable to complaints.'

'If you saw the look on my clients' faces, you wouldn't even be entertaining the idea of complaints.'

'I'm not against foot massages, Martha. Wouldn't mind one myself occasionally. No, it's just the blurring of boundaries thing. Anyway, let's move on.'

Martha was half-grateful to Rob for his frankness in expressing, yet again, his concern about her lack of respect for boundaries, and half-irritated by the pettiness of it.

'Actually, what you've just been saying only stiffens my resolve, Rob. With all this potential for some kind of drama with the Ortons, really, I do think . . . Perhaps it's time . . .'

'Time to retire?'

'The man's a bloody mind-reader.'

'Come on, Martha. It wasn't much of a challenge.'

'Ha. Wouldn't it be brilliant if we really could read minds? That was one of the accusations Abigail Orton hurled at me. That we therapists think we know what's going on in other people's minds.'

'Well, we sort of do. Don't we?'

'Let's not start on that again, okay? Speaking for myself, I only try to give people the space to figure out what's going on in their own minds. I'm a companion on the journey. A guide, maybe. What I mainly offer is a bit of affirmation.'

'Do I detect a subtle shift in the Elliott philosophy? What happened to the therapist as educator? *Leading* them out?'

'Sounds as if I was very boring on the subject. Sorry. I do get passionate. But it's more about *drawing* them out.'

'Let me fill your glass.'

Rob topped up both their glasses and settled back in his chair. 'Okay, then. How far down the track are you with your thinking about retirement? Is it time to talk to Zoe about a more permanent arrangement, do you think? She's always been there when we needed a bit of back-up. I know she's been working for years at another practice as well, but I'm pretty sure she'd like to consolidate all her hours in one place or the other. Actually, if you're serious about this, why don't we offer her a full-time job and maybe even a share of the practice. I suspect she'd jump at the chance. But really, Martha, I'd hate to see you pull out entirely. Clients love you, in case you didn't know.'

'No, it's wind-down time, Rob. And I agree with you about Zoe. Let's have a chat with her and see where her head's at. I've reached the end of the road with three clients in the past few weeks—four if you count the Ortons as a client, which I never really did. Am I willing to take on any new cases? I really don't want to.'

'So what *do* you want to do?'

'Let's talk about that another time, shall we? Get both my knees done, for a start. Can we refocus on the axis of evil?'

'Sure. But we are allowed to ruminate. It's Friday night, remember.'

'Good Lord. You're sounding very mellow, all of a sudden. In fact, come to think of it, you *are* less tense, Rob. Less wound up. I think I'd almost say jaunty. Has there been a development with the Brazilian bombshell, dare I ask? Anything I need to know?'

Rob was not ready for that conversation. He held up his hand. 'Let's get back to you. What sort of timing are you thinking about?'

'This Orton thing has really focused my mind, Rob. I think we should start drawing up a timetable for a pretty swift exit. I'm thinking weeks, not months.'

They lapsed into silence. The late-spring evenings were lengthening and the window of Rob's office was wide open, letting the warmer air blow in. Animated conversation from the back garden of the house next door could be heard—the sound, not the words—and they both smiled.

Rob wanted to be with Samantha. Martha wanted to be at Balmoral. But they were both content to stay where they were, together, for a while longer.

Martha was wrestling with the bigger question, unsure whether it was something she should discuss with Rob. It was Sam she really should talk to, she knew that, but she desperately needed advice about how she might tackle that conversation. About whether she should tackle it at all. Yet the thing she feared most in all the world was that Sam would hear it from someone other than her. The prospect of moving from a few clients to none was trivial—*that* time had come. What she desperately didn't want to have to face, but knew she must, was the possibility that *this* time had come as well.

Yes, she decided. Rob was the right person to discuss it with.

⌒

'So you see my dilemma, Rob. I'd thought Sam would never have to know. Never need to know. Never find out. Her birth certificate has Simon as the father. People often commented that she looked like Simon. Which sort of gave me the creeps, every time I heard it. But it was good for Sam to hear. And for Simon.'

Rob stared at her. Stunned. He couldn't imagine the strain of having to live with something like this for forty years. Carrying it all on her own. No wonder she finally cracked and told *someone*. Far from home, in the arms of Giles . . . It was easy to understand, even if he turned out to have been the worst possible choice of confidant. Rob had no trouble grasping what a disturbing prospect this was for Martha—that Dubois, or Abigail Orton, might find a way to get to Samantha. And for no apparent reason except out-and-out spite. A desire to bring Martha undone. But ten years later? You couldn't even really call it revenge, Rob thought. As far as he knew, Martha had actually been very supportive of Giles, if you overlooked her professional transgression.

It sounded to Rob as if Giles Dubois was no closer to being cured of his psychoses than he was a decade ago. But why was Abigail Orton such a willing accomplice? Could she be so concerned about the wellbeing of her sister that she would risk disrupting the lives of both Martha and Samantha just to give Dubois a moment of . . . what? Euphoria? Satisfaction? It was hard to conceive of the depth of malevolence implied by Abigail's threat. The sheer bloody-mindedness. It only made sense in the context of a serious mental disturbance. This went way beyond irrationality. This was pathological.

His new-found intimacy with Samantha notwithstanding, Rob felt he had no way of knowing how she might react to this news. Couldn't even begin to imagine how he himself might have reacted, if his own mother had broken such news to him at any stage of his life. He only knew that he wished he could be the one to tell Samantha, or at least be present when she was told.

He emptied the bottle, sharing the dregs between them.

'God, Martha. Hell. I really don't know what to say. I get how this happened in the first place. The pregnancy, I mean. I get why you wanted to keep it to yourself. But Samantha? Look, I really don't know. I mean, she's a mature woman and everything, but . . .'

Rob felt the shock as if it were a personal blow. This was *his* Samantha they were discussing. His and Martha's. He desperately wanted to say that, between them, they could love her through whatever trauma she might have to face.

'I've upset you, Rob. This was too much to lay on you. I'm sorry. I shouldn't have told you any of it. I have to work it out myself. I just thought you might—'

'Martha, please. Don't apologise. I'm honoured—truly, that's the word—that you've chosen to share this with me. This is a horrible prospect. On a far bigger scale, obviously, than the other one. In a different league. The question is, was it just a completely hollow threat, designed to put you through exactly what you're now experiencing? Or is there some substance to it? I mean, trying to see it from their point of view, they have more power over you if they *don't* spill the beans to Samantha, so that you have to live with the uncertainty. If Giles, or Abigail Orton and her sister, actually told Samantha, then you'd have to deal with it, and so would she. But they'd lose all their power. Isn't that right?'

'Yes. They'd lose their power over me, and I might well lose my daughter in the process. Who knows what they would say? Who knows how Sam would react? To be told something like this by a total stranger and then having to confront me with it. *Is it true? Why have you kept it from me all my life? Why did you tell that dreadful Giles person but you never told me?* And what would I say? Sam's no fool. If I said it was to protect her, she'd say, *No, Mum, it was to protect yourself.* And she'd be absolutely right. It's true. I lied to my husband, I lied to my daughter, to protect myself. And, of course, I never told Grant he was a father.'

'Well, you didn't actually—'

'I hope you're not going to say I didn't actually lie, Rob. I hope you know that sins of omission are just as bad, just as heinous, as sins of commission. Sometimes worse. As in this case. Oh, no, Rob, don't try to patronise me. Spare me that.'

'Okay, Martha. Fair enough. But let me think about this. I'm sure there's a way to handle this that could work for you *and*

Samantha. And what about Simon? Have you thought about his reaction? Let me spend some time on it. Ponder it a bit.'

In their fifteen years working together, Rob had never seen Martha cry. But here she was, sitting in his office, weeping quietly into a tissue dragged from the box on his desk.

He let her be for some minutes, then said, 'May I give you a hug, Martha? And let's talk again next week. How does that sound? Will you be okay in the meantime?'

A wordless nod from Martha. After the hug, she sat back down in her chair and showed no sign of leaving. She shook her head, as if to clear it of this dark material.

'Send me away on a lighter note, Rob. Tell me some good news. Tell me why you're jaunty. Tell me you've defused the bombshell, at last.'

Rob looked at her, torn between the various versions of this story it might be possible to tell her.

'You're incorrigible, Martha. Relentless. I wish you handled me as gently as you claim to handle your clients. It's a long story. But yes, we've split. Finally and forever. Though Constancia might give you a different version.'

'Oh, Rob. That *is* good news. And Zoe will be delighted too.'

'*Que?*'

'Oh, don't play the innocent with me, Rob. I'm sure she's a wonderful therapist. But, boy, she's hopeless at hiding her feelings for a colleague. And you are a bit of a dreamboat. I can see that. Through half-closed eyes, admittedly.'

'Get out of my office. And have a lousy weekend. I hope the bedbugs *do* bite.'

THIRTY

AFTER THEIR RETURN FROM EUROPE, GILES WAS DULY
admitted to the Neutral Bay clinic, discreetly housed in a gracious
old building that, from the outside, was indistinguishable from
the other houses in the street.

Every weekday morning, Martha would drive over to visit him.
In the beginning, when he was heavily sedated, he appeared to have
no clear idea of who she was, but he was benign enough and able
to make polite conversation. After each visit, Martha would drive
on to Balmoral for lunch and a restorative walk along the sand.

She would drop into the practice occasionally, exchange pleasantries with Sandrine, whose discretion continued to be exemplary
in spite of Martha's temporary retreat from their previous closeness,
and spend a few minutes bringing Rob up to date on the unfolding
saga of Giles. There was nothing about those conversations she
enjoyed. She felt as though she was being exposed as a rather
foolish, naive woman, though Rob never ventured anywhere near
such an assessment. She would also spend a few moments with Zoe,
getting to know her a little better and catching up on the progress

of the clients Martha had handed on to her. Her impression was that Zoe had been an excellent choice of locum.

Giles's psychiatrist was happy enough to speak to Martha, though she was guarded in her responses to Martha's questions. She seemed sympathetic to Martha's situation, but warned her that, in his more lucid moments, Giles was starting to blame Martha for the state he was in. She mentioned several times that Giles had undertaken the trip against her strong advice, and that he had been seeing her twice a week—not once a week as Giles had told Martha—right up until the time of his departure.

In her own defence, Martha claimed to have had no inkling that Giles had been advised not to travel, let alone that such advice might have amounted to a warning. But she had certainly been the prime mover. It was she who was swept up in the idea of the trip and, in retrospect, perhaps she had mistaken Giles's acquiescence for enthusiasm.

But that was all history. Now she had to deal with the reality that Giles was in the care of a competent professional who was being very cautious in her attitude to Martha: reluctant to offer much detail about Giles's condition, and occasionally reminding Martha that she wasn't 'family', and certainly not 'partner'. But she did mention that Giles seemed to have settled into the routine of the clinic as if it were his home. Indeed, she confided in Martha that she was worried by his willingness, even eagerness, to be institutionalised.

~

As the weeks passed, Giles became increasingly lucid, noticeably less anxious, yet more irascible and impatient in his dealings with Martha. He had been moved to the rehab section of the clinic and was functioning more normally than he had been in months. Martha was relieved for him, but acutely aware of his obvious loss of affection for her. A frosty unease had settled on their time together. It was as if they no longer really knew each other, yet Martha still cared deeply about his wellbeing and was pleased by any sign of improvement in his condition. She knew it would have been impossible to separate her devotion from her sense of duty, or even to distinguish duty from some form of compensation for her own feelings of remorse. She was relieved, though, when the psychiatrist advised her to cut back her visits to Mondays and Thursdays.

And then Giles's sister appeared on the scene. Beatrice.

Giles had never mentioned his sister to Martha, and the first she heard of Beatrice's existence was when Martha turned up on a Monday morning for her routine visit to be told by Angela, a nun Martha had always found warm and approachable, that she would not be able to visit Giles today, and perhaps not ever again. Angela was as kind as usual, but firm. She told Martha they had learned from Giles that he had a younger sister in Melbourne and so they had contacted her and explained the situation. Beatrice had arrived on the weekend and spent many hours closeted with Giles, in deep conversation. Temporary accommodation had been arranged for her in the clinic.

'The good news,' Angela said, 'is that Giles seems much more coherent. More fluent. More relaxed. He has shared all his meals with Beatrice and appears generally more cheerful.'

Martha was allowed to meet Beatrice, who was polite but cool. She told Martha that she was well aware of the nature of Martha's 'previous connection' with Giles, she knew all about the Europe trip, and she knew that Martha's relationship with Giles had begun, inappropriately, through their counselling sessions.

She confirmed that Giles had refused to see Martha and she understood that this was to be a permanent ban. She said she was sorry to be the bearer of such news, and hoped it would not be too upsetting.

Then she handed Martha a note from Giles, which Martha opened on the spot. All it said was: *I'll get you for this.* There was no salutation. No signature. No date. But the handwriting was unmistakably his.

Martha had kept that note, along with the poem Giles had written her and a lace handkerchief he had bought her in their first week in Brussels.

With some reluctance, Rob agreed that Martha could see Zoe professionally. It was a bit incestuous, he thought, but Martha had warmed to Zoe enough to feel that she could trust her to be helpful through the period following the final breakdown of Martha's relationship with Giles. She saw Zoe five times over a couple of months, and told her the entire story of her relationship with Giles. Zoe had given her some welcome space for reflection, and encouraged her to express her remorse and regret.

During the months following Giles's refusal to see her, Martha had been almost paralysed by grief. She knew Giles had become a heavy burden, and for much of the time he had seemed no more than that, Yet Martha had invested so much of herself in him that his total rejection of her came as more of a shock than a relief. It was as if she'd been prepared to give up the burden, but not the connection.

When she told her friends the bare bones of the story, they couldn't see any grounds for sadness, let alone grief. They tried to convince Martha that she'd had a lucky escape. When it's over, it's over, was their verdict. While Martha knew that was a perfectly rational response to the situation, she also knew that a big part of her didn't want it to be over at all. She didn't want the complexity, the messiness, the drama, but she sorely missed the intimacy she had once shared with Giles.

Under the gentle guidance of Zoe, Martha gradually came to understand that her grieving over the loss of the Giles she had once loved so intensely was not only as authentic as more conventional kinds of grief, but could be harder to deal with because it wasn't shared, or even really understood by other people. It wasn't legitimised by others' participation in it, or their engagement with it. That insight had helped her to understand why she had been feeling so desolate; so marooned; so alone.

She recalled having had a similar reaction to her two miscarriages, all those years ago. Simon had been bitterly disappointed. Friends had been sympathetic. Yet Martha had had no sense of anyone but herself feeling that those were actual bereavements.

Now Giles had gone. To Martha, it felt as if he, too, were dead; as if this were yet another bereavement. But his note made it clear that Martha was far from dead to him—a thread would continue to connect them, via his desire for revenge for whatever wrong he felt she had done him.

There was yet more to be uncovered. Another kind of grief. With the help of Zoe, Martha was able to acknowledge that she was also mourning the loss of her self-respect—her respect for her own judgement, her respect for the ethical standards of her profession, even her confidence in her ability to care for those wounded souls who might come to her in the future. And, beneath it all, she felt she had spectacularly failed Giles by falling so far short of her own lofty goals when it came to the care of *his* soul.

At their final session, Zoe had said to Martha, 'We're none of us saints, Martha. We're only pilgrims, at best.'

Ten years later, Martha still drew comfort from those words.

THIRTY-ONE

ON SATURDAY MORNING, SAM WAS LAZING IN BED WITH
Rob in the recently restored Crows Nest cottage she used as home
and office. She was still adjusting to the radiance of her new life.
Lying in the arms of a man she adored, who adored her in return,
was an experience she had scarcely dared dream would ever come
her way again; not since the abrupt and never fully explained
breakdown of her last serious relationship, more than five years
ago. The fact that Rob loved her with such tenderness *and* shared
her yearning for parenthood had transported her to an entirely
new realm of being.

'So when are we going to tell your mother?'

Following the previous evening's heavily freighted session
with Martha, Rob felt it was a question he needed to raise again.
The hallmark of his relationship with Samantha, in total contrast to his time with Constancia, was its transparency. They
never hesitated to say what was on their minds. There was no
guile. No dissembling. No prevarication. Honesty and frankness came as easily as breathing. They couldn't imagine any

reason why they would ever want to keep anything from each other.

And now this.

It was Martha's secret, not his, Rob told himself. But now it was in his head, it certainly *felt* like his. Never before had he understood the possible significance of that remark he'd previously regarded as merely cynical: *A problem shared is a problem doubled.*

'Remind me why you're so reluctant to tell Martha about us,' he said. 'Given that we will obviously have to tell her sooner or later. And given that it's good news in every way. I *am* in love with her daughter, after all.'

'I don't know, Rob. Maybe I'm too sensitive to how she might react. You're right, though. We want her to know. She *has* to know. She's going to be a grandmother, for God's sake. We hope.'

Samantha fell silent. She turned and gazed at Rob, but couldn't find the words she wanted. She reached out and traced the line of his jaw with her finger.

'Would a cup of tea help?' he asked.

'Lovely,' she said, and rolled over.

While Rob was making the tea, Sam put on a t-shirt and arranged some extra pillows. She propped herself up and waited. She felt clearer, now, about the reasons for her anxiety over Martha's reaction to the news that her daughter's life had been transformed by Rob's love. (She also had to admit, very reluctantly, and only to herself, that there was another reason why she had been hesitating: she had wanted to be absolutely certain Rob was not on the rebound from Constancia.)

Rob brought mugs of tea with buttered toast on a tray.

'We've never discussed your policy on crumbs in the bed,' he said with a grin. 'So much to learn. So little time.'

'So little time?' Samantha replied. 'I'm forty, not eighty. I feel as if we suddenly have all the time in the world.'

Rob propped himself beside her on top of the bedclothes and, with the plate of toast balanced between them, they sipped their tea.

'Alright, shoot,' Rob said.

'You'll have to bear with me, okay? It's quite hard to articulate. I'm no psychologist, you know.' She took a deep breath. 'Look, I know this might sound silly, but I'm afraid of how our happiness will affect Mum.'

'Really? Affect her in what way?'

'I suspect—I *strongly* suspect—she is a woman who has never been loved. Not really. Not in the way you love me. Not in the way she desperately wanted that awful Giles to love her. *Giles!* That was a fantasy episode if ever I saw one. Did you ever meet him?'

'I never did.'

'Weird. You could tell after being with him for a very short while that he was weird. Intense, but not in a good way. Like a zealot or something. Yet there was my poor mother investing heart and soul in him.'

'That's certainly true. She talked to me about him, after the event, as if he had been all she'd ever dreamed of.'

'*Dreamed of* is right. She needed him to be someone he wasn't. She needed him to be the great love of her life. That was never going to happen. You know Mum, Rob. The enigmatic Martha. I mean, you see her at work, being this wonderful professional counsellor. She's got truckloads of insight into other people's problems, hasn't she? But she couldn't see it. Not in her own case. Is that common? I mean, for counsellors?'

'Maybe a bit of that. But you said the most important thing about it, I think. You said she *needed* him to be the great love of her life.'

'Yes, and that's exactly my point. That's what I'm scared of doing to her. Shoving this—*us*—in her face. Here we are, actually *finding* what she was so desperately seeking. If she's never been loved, how will she feel when she sees me being loved like this by you? I know we have to tell her. And I'm not going to hold back when we do. But can't you see what I'm saying? She could be really upset even while she's genuinely happy for us. I think there's a very sad, very empty part of my mother buried somewhere deep inside, and I don't want to . . . I don't want to be the cause . . . oh, I don't know.'

'Samantha, you're the daughter any mother would dream of having.' Rob put down his mug and leaned over and kissed her. 'Knowing Martha, I imagine she'll be not only content but delighted to see her daughter securely loved. I don't think envy is in Martha's emotional lexicon. Really, I don't.'

'I know that's true. But I'm not talking about envy. I'm talking about something much less conscious than that. God, you're the psychologist. You tell me what I'm trying to say. I just think it might be quite a challenge. That's what I fear, anyway.'

'I get what you're saying. Absolutely. And I guess it's complicated by the fact that she's coming to the end of the road professionally.'

'I know. I thought of that, too.'

'But let's wind back a bit. Forget Giles. Wasn't your dad the love of her life? She once told me they were high-school sweethearts. That sounded pretty good. I've never really understood what went wrong. I gather the divorce was difficult. What divorce isn't?'

'High-school sweethearts. Right. Do you remember *your* high-school sweetheart, Rob? That wasn't the woman you married, was it?'

'Actually, it was. Lasted about five years. No kids. Luckily.'

'There you go. Bad strategy. Children pretending to be grown-ups. I can remember *my* high-school sweetheart. I think he's still in jail. But back then, at seventeen or whatever I was . . . wow. Dangerous stuff. Exciting. Disastrous.'

'Sounds wonderfully lurid. But tell me a bit more about your dad. I don't mean the painful part. I mean, they must have been happy together for some of the time.'

'I was only eighteen when they finally broke up. But it was a horror stretch all through my teens. My father was obviously having a string of affairs—I used to hear him and Mum arguing late into the night when I was trying to study. They stopped sleeping together ages before they actually split. Mum gave me some bullshit story about Dad having insomnia, or snoring, or something. Not that I was interested at the time.'

'So we don't know whether your mother ever did feel really loved. Early on, I mean.'

'No idea. She never talked about it. When I was a kid, I just thought we were a family like any other family. Mum and Dad were just Mum and Dad. I mean, what kid wonders if their parents are madly in love? Too much information.'

'True. But he was a good dad to you?'

Rob was uncomfortably aware that he was deliberately leading the witness. But he thought he detected a glimmer of hope, somewhere in this story, that Samantha might not be as distressed by the news about her biological father as Martha feared.

'I hardly remember. A pretty *absent* father, when I was little. Busy, busy. That's what I mainly remember. Don't disturb your father—he's *busy*. Later on, when I was a teenager, he was mainly an embarrassment, I guess. Especially around my girlfriends. Couldn't help himself. Ogling, mostly. Feigning interest in what they wanted to *do with their lives* after they left school. You can imagine.'

Rob nodded.

'Please don't judge me too harshly when I say this, but I'm going to tell you something I've never told another living soul. Certainly not Mum. I think I actually hated my father a lot of the time. I certainly never felt close to him. He was like a stranger to me. It felt as if he and Mum were adversaries, not lovers. To tell you the truth, I could never understand how they got together in the first place.'

'Maybe in the beginning . . .'

'How would I know? I mean, they both loved *me*, in their very different ways. They both said they did, at least. But I only ever felt it with Mum. She was a dear, dear mother, Rob. When I was growing up, I felt lucky to have her, and I still do. She's a treasure. I'm not nearly as attentive to her as I should be. But I'm sure she knows I love her.'

'That's true. She's often said.'

'Any chance of more tea, waiter?'

Rob went and made another pot of tea. On their growing list of loves and hates in common, they had been childishly delighted by the discovery that they both loathed teabags.

When he returned to the bed, Samantha said: 'I hope that didn't sound too harsh—what I said about my father. I mean, I know he's my father and I suppose there's some kind of bond there. But I can't tell you how relieved I was when he took off for Cairns and then married this woman young enough to be his daughter. He thought I'd be chuffed to have a baby sister. *Half*-sister, anyway. Yeah, sure.'

'Back to Martha for a moment. How can you be certain that she's never been truly loved by a man? I mean, the way she wanted to be. *Never?*'

'I can't be certain, I suppose. Maybe she had a fling with someone she never told me about. Why would she? God—I'm her daughter, not her therapist. Maybe she did have a secret passion. Who knows? But that would be sad, too, wouldn't it? The real point is that I sure as hell never saw any sign of it in her marriage. Once I was . . . I don't know, maybe twelve . . . I only saw the opposite.'

Rob cleared away the mugs and plate and brushed up the crumbs. Then he climbed back under the bedclothes and took Samantha in his arms. An idea was forming in his mind. A plan he thought might satisfy both mother and daughter. He just hated not being able to share it with Samantha.

THIRTY-TWO

BY MONDAY AFTERNOON, MARTHA WAS STRUGGLING TO hold herself together for Ruby's next appointment. It had been a wretched weekend. Gloomy weather. Social isolation, by choice. Discussing any of this with her friends, even the best and closest of them, was out of the question. She had gone endlessly over all the humiliating consequences that could flow from Abigail Orton's double threat. All the nasty possibilities. For her. For Sam. For Simon. Rob had been right about that—Simon would need to be considered, at least. Did he have a right to know? She supposed he might have. *Scenario planning* was what Lucas would probably have called this, and Martha had smiled at the recollection of what she regarded as Lucas's symbolic transition from corporate jargon to more intelligible speech.

But there had been little else to smile about. Martha wondered, for the hundredth time, whether she had been right to confide in Rob, though he was the man she trusted most on earth. And she regarded his neuroses as being well within safe limits, especially now—if she could believe him—that he was free of Constancia's pathogens. *Pathogens?* No, that was unkind. Unworthy. That was no better than the boys in her primary-school playground who had taunted her with talk of *girls' germs*. Martha was prepared to concede that Constancia was probably a sensationally passionate lover, and a perfect companion for someone . . . someone utterly unlike Rob.

Over the weekend, her mind had constantly returned to Giles and the fleeting joys and grinding sorrows of their Brussels odyssey. Such a beautiful city, wrecked for her by his descent into—she couldn't avoid the word—madness. She had recalled that, as part of their daily Grand-Place ritual, Giles had insisted on eating steamed mussels with fries in a paper cone, washed down with Belgian beer. She had known he was not supposed to be drinking, but had hoped the beer might calm him. At least it had not led to any binges. Now she wondered whether he had started drinking again. What interactions that might be setting up with his medication. What his psychiatrist might say if she knew. And then she pulled herself up. She was slipping into Giles fantasyland . . . again.

Still, she couldn't banish from her mind the thought that Giles had apparently latched on to some aspect of their trip that cast her in a very bad light, and had clung to that perception. For ten years? Or was this a fresh revival? And was Abigail Orton's sister now prepared to indulge Giles's every whim, every delusion, every false memory, in order to keep him calm enough to function as a husband? She wished that woman the joy of it.

It was almost time for Ruby. Through the fog of anxiety, distress and confusion, Martha recognised her responsibility to be clear-headed and focused. Every client deserved that. Either she had to cancel the appointment, or rise to the occasion. She had been rising to the occasion for forty years and wouldn't stop now.

Ruby looked like a new woman as she entered Martha's office. Her smile was more generous, more open than the previous tightly rationed version. She was back in her business skirt and jacket, complete with stockings, and showed no sign of wanting to remove her shoes.

Sensing that Ruby was eager to get straight into the conversation, Martha recalled the long, long monologue that had occupied most of their first session together. This time, she had steadied herself sufficiently to be open to Ruby, but she wasn't sure she could handle another onslaught like that one.

As much for her own benefit as Ruby's, she proposed a few breathing exercises as a prelude to their conversation.

When they were relaxed and settled, and the silence had done its work, Martha asked, as she usually did, 'What's been on your mind since we last spoke, Ruby? What would you like to talk about?'

'So. It's hard to know where to begin,' Ruby said. 'I've been doing a lot of thinking. A *lot* of thinking. I've thought a lot more about my conversation with Lucas at your afternoon tea. Even going on the little he said, I'd say his marriage is a far tougher challenge than mine could ever be.'

'In what way?'

'Well, I've been complaining to you about Vince being so *private*—I won't say secretive anymore—but I think Lucas and his wife might be living on different planets. I'd never have said that about Vince and me, in spite of everything. And something Lucas said made we wonder if that dear little boy is actually his. Certainly doesn't *look* like his.'

'Perhaps we might switch the focus for a moment from Lucas to Vincent. You sounded as if you might have been revising your thinking about Vincent. About his therapy, perhaps? About his right to privacy?'

'Oh, there's so much to tell you, Martha. Vince and I have never talked as much as we have in these past couple of weeks.'

'And?'

'Well, you know—this will sound funny—but so much of it was so . . . *private*, I was even wondering whether I should talk to you about it at all. But Vince said, *No. Tell her whatever you like.* So I came back.'

'You've talked to Vincent about our sessions, in the way you wish he'd talk to you about his?'

'Ancient history, Martha.'

'In what way?'

'So, bit by bit, I've been piecing together a very complicated story. It's been hard for Vince to talk about it, because he thought I wouldn't understand. But I think I get it now. I think I do.'

'Ruby, you know you don't have to talk to me about any of this, if you feel uncomfortable, or if you feel we'd be trespassing on Vincent's privacy.'

'No, that's okay. The thing is, we've decided to go ahead and have a baby.'

That warm smile again.

'I might even fall pregnant this week. We'll see.'

Clearly, Martha thought, there were no privacy issues in Ruby's mind.

'Vincent feels you're now well enough established to go ahead?'

'That's the thing, see. It was never about getting well enough established in the sense you mean. The sense I thought it was. Vince wanted to get his *own* house in order.'

'His own house?'

'That's how he put it. He felt he wasn't ready to be a father. And now he is.'

Paternity again, thought Martha. Will this never end? *Focus*, she said to herself sternly, and smiled at Ruby.

'That sounds very promising. Do you want to tell me any more about it?'

'It's fascinating, really. Vince grew up without a father. Like, totally. Gone before Vince was even born. And his mother never re-partnered, so there was no father figure in Vince's life. His grandfather was ancient and he died before Vince started school. No uncles, even. There was a really nice guy who lived next door who used to take Vince to kick a ball in the park with his own kids, and there were a few male teachers who Vince admired. But, up close, no role model at all.'

'You've never mentioned this before.'

'I didn't realise it was such a big deal. Vince never raised it as an issue. Not ever.'

Ruby glanced out the window, then looked straight into Martha's face. She's gathering her courage, Martha thought.

'Anyway, he decided to see this therapist to help him work through all that. He wanted to be sure he was capable of being a true dad. Isn't that awesome?'

It struck Martha that, for once, awesome seemed exactly the right word.

'So we're, like, on the journey. Full steam ahead. *And baby makes three.* Ever see that creaky old movie, Martha? My *grand-mother* loved it. How random is that!'

'It sounds as if you've been through a really joyful experience, Ruby. That you're closer to Vincent than ever.'

'That's true. I feel as if someone's turned the lights back on. So, yeah . . . all good.'

'I'm really pleased for you. And for Vincent. For both of you.'

'Anyway, I haven't finished, Martha. Like: *But wait—there's more!*'

'Do go on.'

'Vince the house-husband. How do you like that? He says my career is more important to me than his is to him, and he thinks one of us should be at home with the child for the first few years, at least. So he wants it to be him.'

'Not a believer in child care?'

'Oh sure, we've talked about that. We're in favour—but not all day, every day, when the child is tiny. Bit of socialisation, sure. But lots of time with a parent, too. Do you know about attachment theory? Well, of course you would. So, anyway, Vince's therapist gives him these journal articles about it and he's sold.'

'And you? Are you sold?'

'Sure I am. I had a better childhood than Vince did, though. I'm one of five, so the household was really chaotic when I was growing up, but in a good way. Lots of love. Lots of laughs. Lots of squabbles, too. Mum was around a lot. She worked, but only part-time. Like, the opposite of Vince and me. It was my dad's career they decided to push. Anyway . . . I think I'm done here.'

'That's lovely, Ruby. I'm delighted to hear you sounding so much more accepting of everything. How is Char reacting to all this, may I ask?'

'Oh, Char. I haven't told her the full story, really. She knows we're trying for a baby. She can find out the rest later. She needs to get to know Vince better. I'll still be seeing plenty of her, of course. She'll be an honorary aunty.'

Ruby picked up her bag and prepared to leave.

'Oh, one other thing. We go to Beauchamp Park every Sunday now. We're just in Middle Cove, so it's only a short drive. That little rubber ball gets a real workout. Awesome.'

That, Martha thought, was possibly a little *less* awesome than Vincent's seismic shift. And then she thought: Who am I to try arranging all the pieces of Ruby's beautiful story into some supposedly rational order of significance? Maybe the rubber ball has played a huge part.

Ruby paused on the way out. 'The scone recipe. I forgot to ask you about it. Has Hazel obliged, or is that a . . . secret?'

'Ah. No, it's not a secret. Hazel says she's been baking scones for so long she just does it without thinking about it. She's going to try to write it down, though. If you don't feel you need to come back, I can post it to you.'

'Post! How quaint. But, yeah, that'd be awesome.'

'So this might be goodbye, Ruby. But you know where to come if you need to. I won't be here so much, but Zoe is wonderful. Or Rob.'

They shook hands. Martha's eyes were glistening, but Ruby didn't notice. She was already rummaging in her bag for her purse, and handing Sandrine her credit card.

Sandrine, eyebrows raised, caught Martha's eye. Cocking her head towards Rob's office, she said: 'Rob would like a word.'

THIRTY-THREE

ROB MOTIONED MARTHA INTO A CHAIR. HE WASN'T SURE he was up to this, but he had to find a way of convincing Martha that what she might regard as one small sin of commission—to use her quaintly pious term—could relieve her of the consequences of what she thought of as a much more significant sin of omission.

'I've slept on it, as promised, Martha. Three sleeps, in fact.'

'I wish I could say the same. Sleep has been rather elusive.'

Looking into Martha's drawn and troubled face, he found it easy to believe she'd lost a lot of sleep over this. A woman as deeply principled as Martha could easily be overwhelmed by remorse. Too easily undone by contemplation of the gap—perhaps the yawning chasm—between the way she'd wanted to live and the way her life had turned out. She talked too easily, he thought, about those sins of omission and commission. It was language she would never use with her clients.

Where would he begin? Respecting Samantha's position was just as important to him as trying to help Martha find a way out of her dilemma.

'Martha, I think I have an idea that could help. Let me explain.' He looked at his watch. 'Would you like a drink? I know it's not Friday, but it is well past six.'

'I think I'd rather just hear what you have to say, Rob. Dear Rob. You must know that I feel wretched over this. My beautiful Sam. The one person in the world I'd hate to hurt. Even to upset. Why should she have to find out that her mother . . . well, you know what her mother did.'

'Actually, I've had a couple of conversations with Samantha over the past couple of months. She opened up quite a bit when we had that lunch at Oscar's, after your little high-tea caper.'

Martha let 'little' and 'caper' pass. And it wasn't 'high tea', either.

'You don't mean Sam has been seeing you professionally?'

'No, no, nothing like that. But we've met a few times for coffee and she's clearly needed to get some stuff off her chest.'

Rob thought: Oh, how it pains me to tell such a tiny part of the truth.

Martha thought: Zoe wouldn't like to know he's having coffee with a gorgeous young woman, even if she is only my daughter.

'It's just that she's said a few things about her life with you and Simon that make me realise she might not be as disturbed by this information as you fear.'

'Oh, come on, Rob. You can't know that. What sort of things has she been saying?'

'Well, it won't surprise you to hear that she's far from devoted to Simon. And that's putting it mildly.'

'Go on.'

'And—look, Martha, she might not like me telling you this, but I think she feels terrible regret, on your behalf, that Simon didn't turn out to be the love of your life.'

'Pah! What a romantic she is. Not the love of my life? *Simon?* No shit, Sherlock, as Sam herself used to say. Where are you going with this, Rob? Cut to the chase, for goodness' sake.'

'Okay. I think I know how you can tell Samantha the truth in a way that will soften the blow. Make it less brutal.'

'Go on, Rob. This is like pulling teeth.'

'I think if you told her that her biological father *was* a grand passion—well, maybe not quite that, but at least tell her he was someone you had a serious love affair with—it would make a huge difference. If you felt able to say that Geoff . . . Greg . . . What was his name?'

'Grant.'

'Grant. But actually, it would be better not to give him a name. Let's not start another magical mystery tour, searching for the real father . . .'

'Quite. Go on with this elaborate fantasy.'

'Well, that's it, basically. Tell Samantha that she was the product of an intense, passionate affair, but that you were already married to Simon, and this other man had a wife and kids, so it was just an impossible situation. You parted company with great sadness and you never even told him you were pregnant. That's an important part of the story.'

'Which also happens to be true.'

'So it becomes a classic romantic tragedy, Martha. Which it almost was.'

'You want me to lie to my own daughter about my feelings towards her biological father?'

'No, I want you to admit to yourself, and also to Samantha, that you had an affair. Even if that would be stretching the truth a bit—and it might not be—I thought you were already lying to her on a far bigger scale than that.'

Martha's chin fell to her chest. 'I don't think I could do that,' she said.

'Martha, listen. Before you write off the idea, put yourself in Samantha's shoes. Okay? She has hostile feelings towards Simon. She's saddened by the thought that you might never have had enough passion, enough romance in your life. Not Simon. Not Giles—oh yes, she's mentioned Giles to me. What would she rather hear: that her mother had a one-night stand at a conference with some random bloke for whom she felt nothing but passing lust? Or—here's the alternative version—that her mother had a passionate, exhilarating affair that was doomed from the start because of the complications in the lives of both parties? It's not *Romeo and Juliet*, but it's not bad. And it's not completely untrue. It's an . . . embellishment. An embroidery of the truth, to borrow my late mother's turn of phrase. To protect your daughter's feelings, Martha. This is for Samantha's sake, not yours.'

'Certainly not mine.'

'Think of it as a sacrifice you can make in the interests of Samantha's happiness. Her mental wellbeing, if you like. You haven't invented a father. This is the real father. Grant. Okay, it's a slightly romanticised version of the story. But *how* romanticised? How do I know—how do *you* know, after all these years? Forty years. Do you remember exactly how you were feeling? There was passion there, surely, no matter how fleeting. You don't have to tell Samantha how fleeting. You felt *something* for this guy. How can you be sure you haven't diminished the significance of it in your own mind, just so you can excuse it as nothing more than a reckless one-night stand? Forty years ago? I wouldn't like to swear how I *really* felt—at the time—about some of the people I slept with even *twenty* years ago.'

'He was an ageing roué.'

'Martha, I would strongly urge you not to say *that* to his biological daughter. And, anyway, there you go again. I think you might be trying to let yourself off the hook by pretending you felt nothing for this guy. Maybe you did. Maybe you didn't. But I sure as hell wouldn't be so certain, if I were you. It's become a convenient narrative in your mind, Martha. A cliché, to be blunt. A neat way of framing what happened. So reframe it! Rewrite the narrative!'

Rob jumped out of his chair and began pacing the room. 'Forty years ago? The guy is probably dead by now, or propped up in a nursing home. Maybe consoling himself with the memory of those idyllic few days he spent in Adelaide with the young and reckless Martha Elliott. Maybe he's carried a torch for forty years. Your face says you don't think so. How would you know? Give your daughter a break, Martha. Let this man be someone she can think of fondly. The man who *really* loved her mother, even if only briefly.'

'It's a lie, Rob. All your fancy embroidery can't disguise the fact that it's a lie.'

'Is it, Martha? *Is it?* Tell me how Grant treated you the morning after.'

Long pause. 'Actually, we went to bed three nights in a row. I was too embarrassed to tell you that before. I was mad. Not madly in love, Rob. Just mad. Reckless, yes. Desperate, maybe. Grant certainly treated me with a tenderness Simon never displayed.'

Rob shrugged and held out his hands, palms up.

'At least give this some thought, Martha. At least consider it from Samantha's point of view.' Rob began to pace again. 'There is an alternative,' he said. 'You could wait for the evil axis to contact Samantha and tell her the story in the most sordid terms possible. Then she could come to you for confirmation, and you could deny the whole thing.'

'That would be an even worse lie. A far worse lie. I think I prefer your version.'

'Or you *could* say: *Yeah, it's all true. Guilty as charged. You're the child of an illicit, dirty, meaningless humiliation.*'

'Oh, Rob. You remind me of Sam sometimes. You really do. So over-the-top. Yet so . . . I hate to say it . . . so *persuasive* . . . so *plausible.*'

'I know it's tricky. I know it goes against the grain. But you're doing your daughter a favour. Think of it that way. You'll be minimising the inevitable shock. It will still be a shock. I'm not saying it won't. But do you want to go on feeling as miserable as you are now? Do you want Giles Dubois and the Ugly Sisters to have this power over you indefinitely?'

'What do you think?'

'You know your daughter better than I do. You decide which version you'd like her to live with. And don't tell me only one of them is true. It's never that simple, Martha. You know that. Three nights, eh?'

'Don't rub it in, you smug little bastard. There *is* a hint of smugness about you since you shed the dreaded *In*constancia. You're looking far too pleased with yourself, Rob. Anyway, I'm grateful you've given this so much thought.'

'And I'll just say one other thing. Aren't *you* grateful to Grant for giving you Samantha? Doesn't that count in his favour?'

Martha stood and they embraced briefly.

'I'm on your side,' Rob said. '*And* Samantha's.'

THIRTY-FOUR

'SAM? IT'S ME.'

'Hi, Mum. What's up?'

'How does your diary look this week? Any days that could be free?'

'Let me check. What's this about?'

'Don't laugh, but I have a sudden urge to take a ride on a Manly ferry. Haven't done it for about twenty years, I'd say. I watch them sail past Balmoral all the time and I want to be on one again.'

'You want me to come on a *ferry ride* with you?'

'Not just *any* ferry ride. A Manly ferry. And no, not *just* that. I thought we could drive to Manly, park the car and take the ferry to Circular Quay. Have lunch in town, do a bit of shopping, maybe, then catch the ferry back to Manly before peak hour. What do you think?'

'*Shopping?*'

'I know. Doesn't sound like me. Well, we could just have a walk in the Botanic Gardens. Haven't done that for yonks, either.'

'What is this, Mum? A girls' day out, all of a sudden?'

'Kind of. Yes. I've been busy. You've been busy. Why not spend a day together?'

'I'll look at the calendar. Can I call you back?'

⁓

They had settled on Wednesday for the ferry ride. Sam had an appointment in the city that morning, so she arranged to meet Martha at Circular Quay, have lunch together and perhaps a walk in the gardens, then join her on the ferry back to Manly. It sounded to Sam a bit like a school excursion, minus the visit to an art gallery or museum.

She sat at an outside table at City Extra, with the Manly ferry wharf nearby. When she saw Martha's ferry approaching, she paid her bill and walked to the exit barriers. She couldn't remember the last time she'd stood like this, waiting to catch sight of her mother in a public place.

The spring sales were on in the city stores, and a gaggle of shoppers were mingling with assorted daytrippers and people heading for appointments in the city with medical specialists, financial advisers, travel agents, divorce lawyers. The faces ranged from playful to grim, some hidden behind the face masks that, post-Covid, many people had taken to wearing routinely.

When Sam caught sight of Martha, she experienced a moment of heartbreak. Her mother had tried to dress for a day out. A hopelessly unfashionable floral skirt Sam hadn't seen for years. A far-from-pristine green linen jacket. A straw hat that looked more suitable for weeding gardens than strolling in them. A slash of lipstick that was both uncharacteristic and unsuitable. My poor mother, Sam thought. Why is she trying so hard? I'm only her daughter, for God's sake. A surge of the deepest affection swept her towards her mother, but it was mingled with mild concern. Was Martha starting to lose her grip?

They hugged briefly and Martha smiled. 'Just as lovely as I'd hoped it would be. Quite rough crossing the heads, but that's part of the experience, isn't it? The harbour trips are so boring by comparison. And there were such *interesting* people on board. Just listening to all the different accents. A lot of tourists, I think.'

Again, Sam felt that little twinge of concern. Why is she trying so hard? It struck her that her mother seemed nervous. Was there more to this girls' day out than Martha had implied? Was there bad news? A health issue? Not dementia, surely.

Sam took her mother's arm and they walked past the Opera House and on towards the Queen Elizabeth gate to the Botanic Gardens. Martha spotted a bench and suggested they sit for a moment.

'I don't know what I was thinking about, suggesting a walk in the gardens. My knees aren't up to it. Do you mind if we just sit here for a while? Maybe have lunch somewhere down here at sea level?'

'Let's go to the restaurant on the roof of the Customs House. We can take the lift. How's that?'

'Perfect. Thanks, Sam. I feel a bit feeble, though. I had such grand plans.'

They sat for some minutes in silence, surveying the Wednesday sailors competing on the harbour and the people strolling along the pathway where they were sitting. It was a sparkling day to be out. Sam's anxiety eased a little. Perhaps Martha had simply wanted the nostalgic thrill of a ferry ride on such a day.

Eventually, Martha announced that she was hungry and they should head for the restaurant. Again, Sam took her arm and could feel Martha's need of it.

Martha had wondered whether it might be best to raise the subject with Sam over lunch, so the ferry trip back to Manly could be a kind of denouement. But even though the tables at Cafe Sydney were well spaced, Martha felt it was not the place for such a private conversation.

Over lunch, Sam brought Martha up to date with the progress of her business, and sounded enthusiastic. Martha's pride in her daughter had grown with the years. She hadn't approved of some of her choices of boyfriend—none of them, actually—but, in all other ways, Sam had been a continuing source of wonderment to her mother. Martha was determined not to mention the sperm-donor question unless Sam raised it. The brief reference over the phone suggested there might be a pause. Or even some rethinking. Martha hoped so.

⁓

Sam paid the bill and they walked slowly back to the wharf to wait for the next ferry.

Martha still seemed tense, and Sam wondered again if there was bad news coming.

When the *Narrabeen* pulled into the wharf and they watched the passengers disembarking, Martha's spirits seemed to rise, and Sam's concern eased.

'Upper or lower deck, Mum?' she asked, when it was their turn to board the ferry.

'I can't do the stairs, Sam. But let's sit outside.'

When they were settled, Martha said: 'This ferry's past its use-by date, you know. Bit like me.'

'Oh, Mum,' Sam said. Perhaps retirement was the subject of whatever serious discussion was looming. She was now quite sure there was one.

Martha had always felt a particular sense of anticipation as the crew prepared the old Manly ferries for departure. A sense of adventure. Perhaps it was the impressive bulk of the vessels themselves. Perhaps it was knowing they would be crossing the heads. A taste of the open sea. A greater vulnerability to wild coastal weather than was the case for the inner-harbour ferries that never had to deal with more than a bit of chop or occasional fog.

Today was sunny with a stiff breeze, enough to keep the Wednesday yachties busy. Martha was hoping for the same kind of swell that had added some excitement to her morning journey.

The engine throbbed, the gangways clanked, ropes were whipped off bollards and the journey began. Initially held in check by the speed limit in Circular Quay, they rounded Bennelong Point and the soaring concrete sails of the Opera House, then gathered speed as they passed Fort Denison and headed into the main channel for the run to the heads.

Martha wondered when would be the best moment. She noticed Sam was dozing beside her, her head tipped forward.

As they passed Bradleys Head, Martha nudged Sam awake and said: 'I have something to tell you. I don't know whether you'll think it's good or bad. But I need to tell you anyway.'

Here it comes, thought Sam, conscious that she was a little fuzzy from her nap. She wasn't getting as much sleep as usual. The nights were too exciting for sleep. She looked into her mother's face for a clue but couldn't find one.

Martha took her hand, which slightly alarmed Sam.

'I've become a bit of a lame old duck, Sam. I know that about myself. Not in years, necessarily. But look at me. You wouldn't think I was once . . . well, would you?'

'Oh, Mum, what are you on about? You're not even seventy. Don't go all pathetic on me. Have your knees fixed. Lose a few kilos. Buy a new wardrobe. Get a spunky haircut. You'll be back in business before you know it.' Sam smiled tentatively at her mother, hoping this was just an uncharacteristic bout of self-pity. 'I know you were young and gorgeous,' she said. 'I've seen the photos.'

There was a pause.

'I don't know about gorgeous,' Martha said, glad of the opening, 'but when I was young—much younger than you are now, Sam; mid-twenties . . . Well, this is what I wanted to tell you. Back then, when I was that age, I met a man—a man who loved me like I'd never been loved before.' Martha had thought carefully about those words, and decided they were literally true.

'Mid-twenties? You were already married to Dad?'

'I was.'

'Do I need to know this?' Sam asked, now fully awake. Alert. Bolt upright in her seat. Checking no one else was within earshot. 'Are you saying you were *both* unfaithful? Why the hell are you telling me this? Please don't fill my head with extraneous information about your love-life.'

'It's just that your father . . .'

'And don't talk to me about Dad, either. I know your marriage was a sham. Obviously. Cairns is welcome to him and his little love nest. Change the subject.'

'Just, well, see, I *was* loved in a way Simon could never love me.' Another careful choice of words.

'Okay, Mum. I get it. The love of your life was not the man you were married to. It happens. But you stuck to your marriage. Not sure why.'

'Sam, to be more precise, this happened forty years ago. Do you understand what I'm saying?'

Sam stared at Martha for a moment, then jumped out of her seat and ran up the stairs to the upper deck and found a spot at the very front, away from other passengers in the open area overlooking the bow, where she could stand with the wind streaming through her hair. They were starting to cross the heads now, and the strong swell was causing the ferry to pitch and roll, sending spray flying as the bow thudded into each trough. Sam wanted spray on her face. Wanted it to *sting*.

She was breathing heavily, almost panting. This was not like anything she had ever experienced. She wasn't shocked, exactly. She was surprised, certainly, to learn this about her mother. But not shocked. One of her own lovers—the only one she had ever wanted to have children with—had been a married man. To learn that Simon, a person she had come to despise, was not her biological father, came as a . . . relief? No, not exactly. A very dramatic twirl of the kaleidoscope, though. A radical rearrangement of the facts of her life. Neither welcome nor unwelcome. Radical.

But why had her mother waited until now to tell her this? And, having waited so long, why tell her at all? It was as though she'd lived her life under a veil that her own mother had suddenly torn off. Oh, so *this* is who I am.

Part of her—a very small part—admired her mother for finding the courage to say the words, except she hadn't really said them at all. It was more like, *draw your own conclusions, Sam.* Part of her wanted to hate her mother for those forty years of deception. Part of her wanted to wail. Part of her wanted to laugh. Part of her wanted to pretend it wasn't true.

All of her wanted to share this with Rob.

She was not who he thought she was. Not who *she* thought she was. Yet here she was. Herself, still. Unchanged. She had always been the daughter of an unknown father. Her mother had always been a woman disappointed in love. Nothing had changed. Except that now she *knew*. That had changed. That had changed everything, it suddenly seemed, while changing nothing. *Paradox* was one of Rob's favourite words. He'll love this one, she thought. She hoped.

Robin Nielsen. She said his name aloud. He seemed the only fixed point in her life at this moment. The only stable, unchanged, unchanging thing. The only solid thing. In the face of all this, Rob was still reliably, solidly Rob. Her father was not her father. Her mother was an adulterous deceiver . . . *and* . . . the mother who had borne her, raised her, loved her, supported her through everything she'd done. The good, the bad, the downright stupid.

Okay.

You're forty, Sam said to herself. Not twenty. And he *was* a real live lover, after all. Not an anonymous sperm donor.

❧

On the lower deck, Martha sat waiting. If she ever wanted to do away with herself, she decided, it would be by throwing herself overboard from a Manly ferry at night—though her knees would have to be in better shape than they were now if she were to clamber over the railing. Then she thought of sharks and concluded that it was not such a good idea, after all.

The swell was abating. She had deliberately chosen to sit on the port side so that, as the ferry passed Middle Head, she would be able to look at . . . yes, there was her beloved Balmoral Beach, though this was not how she imagined she might be feeling when she had dreamed of being, once again, on one of those ferries she had watched from the shore.

❧

Sam slowly descended to the lower deck. The ferry was already entering Manly Cove and approaching the wharf. People were gathering their belongings and preparing to disembark. She sat beside Martha and took her hand again.

Neither of them said a word until they were off the ferry. Walking along The Corso towards the parking station where Martha had left her car, Sam said: 'I want an ice cream. Will you have one, too?'

'*Some* things never change,' Martha said.

They bought ice-cream cones then continued to walk until they found a bench overlooking the beach. They talked about trivial subjects as they sat and watched the surfers and board-riders.

It wasn't until they were sitting in the car that Sam said: 'Before we start driving, please tell me everything you can about this man. Except his name. I don't want to know his name and I don't want to know whether he's alive or dead. Just tell me . . . did he have an exciting creative streak? Was he courageous? Passionate? Wise, but a bit reckless, too? Tell me he treated you kindly. Tell me you parted as friends. And I bet he was another psychologist. Am I right?'

Sam saw Martha's eyes fill with tears and then overflow. That was all the answer she needed.

⁓

As soon as Martha had dropped her off at home, Sam was on the phone.

'Babe? I have some rather surprising news. I think I need you to take me out somewhere to dinner.'

Rob smiled into the phone. 'That isn't surprising news.' Keep it cheeky. Keep it light.

'No, you nitwit. I mean I want you to take me out to dinner so I can *tell you* some rather surprising news.'

'Good or bad?' he asked.

'It's not that simple. But I need to tell you in person.'

'Okay. I can be away from here by six, so I'll see you as soon as the traffic allows. We can walk up to Willoughby Road and you can decide what you feel like eating when we get there.'

'See you when I see you. I think I love you more than ever, if that's possible. I certainly *need* you more than ever. Does that sound a bit desperate? Sorry.'

Rob put the phone down on his desk. The tone of Samantha's voice told him she was shaken but still strong. Still herself. Positive. *Well done, Martha Elliott*, he said to the empty room.

THIRTY-FIVE

A MONTH HAD PASSED. HAZEL HAD SENT A MESSAGE, VIA Sandrine, to say that she was too busy to make any more appointments for the time being. Lucas had also cancelled a couple more appointments, and Martha was ready to draw a line under both cases, as she already had with Ruby. Now there were just two long-term clients she was still seeing sporadically, and she was preparing to hand both of them on to Zoe.

'I guess this is called *easing* into retirement,' she had said to Rob. She didn't need one of Ruby's flow charts to lay it out for her. Sandrine had been briefed to assign all new cases to Zoe, who was thriving on her increased involvement in the practice. It only remained for Martha to name the date of her departure and set up a meeting with their lawyer and accountant to arrange the sale of her half of the practice to Zoe.

And then another message came from Hazel, this one inviting Martha to have afternoon tea at Hazel's flat with her and Felix, 'and a few others', to be joined later by Lucas. It was to be a small celebration of Hazel's eightieth birthday. No gifts. The subtext, according to Sandrine, was that although Hazel and Lucas were no longer Martha's clients, they did not want to lose contact with the person who had brought them together.

⁓

Martha had no trouble identifying the door of Hazel's flat—a single red balloon was tied to the handle. In spite of Hazel's instructions, she had brought a modest gift—a box of macaroons from Oscar's.

Hazel answered the door, but was pushed aside by Felix, rushing to greet Martha and hugging her around the legs. 'Marfa, Marfa,' he said enthusiastically, 'it's Hazy's birfday. *Look!*'

'Come in, dear,' Hazel said. 'He's still having trouble with his *th* sound. We're working on it, but you'll have to settle for being Marfa for now. He remembers you from our little visit to Beauchamp Park. And Ruby, too.'

Hazel was flushed. Smiling. Pleased to be eighty. Looking and sounding years younger than when Martha had first met her. Martha handed her the box of macaroons, assuring her it was a contribution to the afternoon tea, not a birthday gift.

The bond between Hazel and Felix was a delight for Martha to behold. Felix talked nonstop, which Martha had thought was Hazel's specialty, but it was clear the older woman had met her match in the young boy. Decorations, clearly made by Felix, festooned the living room—paper chains, streamers, stars and assorted drawings, mostly in red. 'They're all supposed to be of me,' Hazel said with pride. A sheet of paper bearing a child's red handprint was stuck to the door of the fridge, visible in the kitchen adjacent to the dining area. On the small dining table sat a large cake.

Two women about Hazel's age were preparing food in the kitchen. They, too, seemed high on Felix's list of favourite people.

A knock sounded, and Hazel and Felix admitted two more guests: Bill and Ruby. A shock ran through Martha at the sight of Bill Orton. Boundary-hater though she was, she was now being made acutely aware of the risk she had taken in organising those little afternoon teas with clients, though none had previously led to further social contact involving her. Still, an eightieth was surely an exception.

Bill, sensing her awkwardness, tried to put her at ease: 'I'm on my own these days, Martha. A very long and ugly chapter is behind me. I'll buy you a cup of coffee sometime, if you're up for it.'

Martha knew she would never be up for it.

Ruby's eyes were shining. She shook Martha's hand and simply said, 'All good.'

Two other guests arrived—a young man Hazel introduced as her neighbour and a woman in her fifties, bearing a beautiful bouquet, who turned out to be Hazel's GP.

Martha decided to focus on the guests who were not former clients. Felix reinforced that decision by attaching himself to Martha while Hazel was busy circulating with food and drinks, backing her into an armchair with a pile of books under his arm. 'Let's read books,' he said, climbing onto her lap. Martha inserted a cushion between Felix and her knees, to minimise the pain.

Several of the books in the pile were familiar to Martha from Sam's childhood. What a long life *The Very Hungry Caterpillar* has had, she thought. And here was *Green Eggs and Ham* still going strong. And *Thomas the Tank Engine*, of course.

Story time was interrupted by the singing of 'Happy Birthday', the cutting of the cake, and Hazel's determination not to make a speech, expressed so vehemently and at such length, it amounted to a speech. The essence of it was that she was grateful that everyone was here, particularly Felix—a special mention that offended no one.

Some guests chose to sit in the small courtyard, beside the empty splash pool that had pride of place. Others remained in the kitchen or at the dining table. There were only two other armchairs in the living area, and Martha was relieved they were occupied by the two women who had been preparing the food, Joyce and Edwina (from the now-defunct garden club, Edwina said). They were deep into gossip and showed no interest in Martha.

The pile of books was finally read, which was the signal for Felix to ask for them all to be read again. Martha obliged with great willingness. Reading books to a child turned out to be a great escape, in more ways than one. Hazel glanced approvingly in their direction a few times. At some point, Felix fell asleep, and when Martha finally noticed, she let her voice taper off into a murmur. She stayed put, surprised by what a comfort it was to have, once again, a small body nestled against her.

After ninety minutes or so, people started to leave, some clutching a piece of birthday cake wrapped in a paper napkin. There were bursts of laughter. But still Felix slept. Martha waved silently to the departing guests. Ruby touched her gently on the shoulder and said a hushed goodbye. Bill gestured to say he would call her, and Martha smiled noncommittally.

As Bill was leaving, Lucas arrived. Martha noted a warmth between the two men as they shook hands that suggested they might well have been in touch since they had met at her afternoon tea. Lucas smiled at Martha, who still had the sleeping child on her lap, and mouthed a silent 'hello'. He greeted Hazel with a hug and a kiss, and handed her a beautifully wrapped gift. 'The shop wrapped it,' he said, as if to distance himself from anything so elaborately and carefully done. Or perhaps to be sure he wouldn't be given credit for it. Martha found that curiously touching.

At the sound of his father's voice, Felix awoke, scrambled off Martha's knee and ran to Lucas. 'Barf now, Daddy?'

Martha struggled to her feet and said she must be off, not wanting to be caught up in the intimacy of bathtime.

'More stories, Marfa,' Felix demanded.

'Next time, Felix,' Hazel said.

Martha heard herself agreeing, and possibly meaning it.

Lucas saw her to the door and, for something to say, Martha asked after Rani. It would have seemed impolite, she thought, not to have mentioned his wife.

'Okay, I think,' was all Lucas offered in reply. He wasn't smiling as he said goodbye and closed the door.

⁓

As Martha was attending Hazel's party, texts were being exchanged between the twin sisters.

Hi Gabs.
Mission accomplished. Just checked. No more
appointments being accepted for Elliott. Retired.
Vanished. Vanquished. And we still have the daughter
up our sleeve. Justice at last!
Abs xox

> *The witch is dead! Joy unconfined. Himself grinning*
> *ear to ear. Not sure he fully gets the import but he's*
> *into the bubbles. And my pants, of course. The man is*
> *an addict.*
> *Gabs xox*

Spare me the shag-brag, Gabs. He cdnt be addicted to
a nicer gal. Anyhoo . . . two birds with one stone.
A win for Giles and the boot for Billy. Talk tonight?
Or go out somewhere?
Abs xox

THIRTY-SIX

MARTHA LIVED IN A 1930S BLOCK OF FLATS ON THE EASTERN side of the railway line, close to Roseville station. She had moved there with Sam as soon as the family home in Gordon had been sold, post-divorce. Half the proceeds of the sale had been more than enough for Martha to buy herself this flat and put a sizeable sum of cash on term deposit. She assumed Simon's share would have made little impact on his already-swollen coffers.

The flat had two bedrooms, one still kept for Sam to stay overnight whenever she wished—which, these days, was never. Bur Martha insisted she keep a key, just in case. There was a small balcony facing east where Martha liked to sit when she was in pensive mode—as she was on this warm Sunday morning in late spring . . .

. . . *Chicago's not such a bad place to be, after all, as long as you've learned to forgive. Especially if you've learned how to forgive yourself . . .*

. . . *Better, far better, for Sam to know the truth, even if the impetus for telling it had come from a place of such malevolence.*

I sometimes find myself feeling curiously grateful to Abigail and her co-conspirator. Abby and Gabby. What were their parents thinking? . . .

. . . I might try to write up the Orton case in detail one day. Or maybe not. Some things better left unsaid . . .

. . . Poor Giles. I guess I'll never know how that marriage will turn out. I wish them well, though I fear it's a doomed enterprise. But I hope I'm wrong. I really do. And Abigail? She's lost a husband who seemed a good man. Will she now succumb to the corrosive power of her own despair, cloaked in bitterness, anger and resentment? Classic case of someone who could really benefit from therapy but lacks the insight to realise she needs help and the courage to go find it . . .

. . . I'm grateful, and rather amazed, that things seemed to have settled down so quickly with Sam, though I do notice she's a little less forthcoming than usual. Perhaps a little more secretive. Strange that she's only ever asked me one follow-up question: Does Dad know? I was able to assure her that he did not—though I didn't admit that was because I hadn't got around to deciding how to handle that particular challenge. He couldn't handle it, was all she had said. Not quite sure what she meant by that . . .

. . . Some things have become clear. I'll retire on Christmas Eve. Sandrine's just turned sixty-five, and she's decided to retire, too, just as soon as she's found a replacement for herself. Her husband wants to travel; Sandrine wants to spend more time with her grandchildren. I'm staying right out of that . . .

. . . I can feel myself being recruited into the role of honorary aunt to dear little Felix. And what if Sam succeeds in her mission, one way or another? Will there be two littlies entering my life? Better get the knees done . . .

⁓

Martha's leafy morning view was brightened by patches of purple, where jacarandas and wisteria were still in bloom. The familiar rattle of trains was a reassuring background noise—she had ridden those trains to school, and then to university, and then to work. Now she drove everywhere.

It was a two-storey block; eight flats. Martha's was at the rear, on the upper level. Just fourteen stairs, in two flights separated by a landing, but they were an increasing challenge to Martha's knees. She took the steps in easy stages, and tried to limit her comings and goings to once a day. The building's security system meant that visitors had to buzz from the main entrance. Martha's flat also had its own security screen door with a bell.

That bell was now ringing. Sam never arrived unexpectedly these days, so some opportunist must have snuck through the entrance while someone else was being buzzed in. It happened.

⁓

The previous night, over dinner, Rob had proposed to Samantha.

It had taken a moment for the words to register. Rob's tone of voice hadn't changed, and he had made the question sound like part of the flow of an inconsequential conversation they were having about something they'd heard on the evening news. When she realised what he had just said, Samantha dropped her cutlery and buried her face in her hands. Laughing. Crying. Both at once.

After a moment, she got up from her chair and threw herself onto Rob's lap. 'Thank you for not going down on one knee,' she said. 'Thank you for not buying a ring without consulting me on the design. Thank you for being the loveliest man in the known universe.'

More laughter. More tears.

She buried her face in Rob's shoulder as he stroked her back.

Eventually, he asked, 'May I have an answer?'

Samantha sat upright on his lap, leaned back and looked him in the eye. 'Are you serious? Do I really have to answer the one question I had hardly dared to hope you might ask me?'

'You do. I need a firm, clear response.'

Samantha yelled, 'YES!' at the top of her voice. She repeated it in a whisper, and kissed Rob on the lips.

'There's no way I would have presumed to choose a ring without even knowing what you might say,' he said.

'Well, I can't imagine you doubted what I might say, but I would like to be there when we buy the ring.'

'So you *do* want a ring?'

Samantha yelled again: 'YES!' Then she grinned and said, 'Of course I want a bloody ring, you sap. I'm a traditionalist through and through when it comes to rings, weddings, changing my name, having babies . . .'

Samantha paused and frowned. 'I was going to tell you something over dinner tonight, babe. Not such good news, I'm afraid. My period came. So we wait another month.'

'I'm kind of pleased, strangely,' Rob said. 'The last thing I'd want you to think is that I only wanted to marry you because we were expecting our baby. Baby or no baby, I want you to be my wife, Samantha Elliott. *Ahem* . . . till death us do part.'

'Sounds like a hell of a long time . . .'

'Forever.'

They kissed again.

'Rob?'

'Samantha?'

'I think we should tell Martha. Now. Tomorrow. In the morning. If she assumed I could handle the truth about my father, I think we should assume she can handle this.'

'And I want her to know that this has got nothing to do with babies.'

'Nothing?'

'You know I'd love us to have a child together. But I want to marry you, regardless.'

'That's all I need to hear.'

⸺

Martha opened the door to her two favourite faces in all the world. Both grinning at her like children bursting with news. A bottle of champagne held aloft.

'We're not here to toast the new grandmother, in case you're wondering,' Sam said. 'We're here to toast the mother of the bride-to-be.'

'Rob? You and *Sam*?'

'Yep.'

'Not Zoe?'

'Zoe? You'd make a hopeless detective, Martha. It was never Zoe.'

Rob as her son-in-law? Martha could hardly imagine a more pleasant prospect, from every point of view.

'Well, then,' she said, beaming with the sudden joy of it, 'you'd better come in and share your grand plans with me.'

ACKNOWLEDGEMENTS

CONSULTANT PUBLISHER
Richard Walsh

JUNIOR COMMISSIONING EDITOR
Tom Bailey-Smith

COPYEDITOR
Ali Lavau

PUBLISHING ASSISTANT
Allegra Bonetto

PROOFREADER
Pam Dunne

COVER DESIGNER
Mika Tabata

PUBLICIST
Rosie Scanlan

No author could wish for a more talented, sensitive, committed and professional team to work with than this one. I am grateful to them all for the support, encouragement and guidance I have received throughout the evolution of *The Therapist*.

I am also grateful to Don Mackay and Stephanie Wells for their thoughtful responses to the first draft of the book and, as ever, to my wife, Sheila, for her constancy in support of my writing. The book is gratefully dedicated to her.